The Black Books of Elverum

The Black Books of Elverum

Mary S. Rustad
editor and translator

2009
Galde Press, Inc.
Lakeville, Minnesota, U.S.A.

The Black Books of Elverum

Printed in U.S.A.

First Edition, 1999
First Trade Softcover Edition, 2006
Third Printing, 2008

The two *Svartebøker* from Rustad were first translated from Gothic handwriting into modern typescript by Per Sande. The two books were then translated from Old Norwegian into modern Norwegian by Per Holck, M.D., Ph.D. Finally, Mary S. Rustad translated the two books from Norwegian to English with the helpful guidance of the late Oskar Garstein, Doctor of Theology and Philosophy.

Illustrations of Jesus and Lucifer by E. T. Rustad

Illustrations by Theodor Kittelsen from Anon. *Theodor Kittelsen.* Oslo: Gyldendal Norsk Forlag, 1945.

Library of Congress Cataloging-in-Publication Data
Svartebøker. English.
The black books of Elverum / Mary S. Rustad, editor and translator.
p. cm.
Includes index.
ISBN 1-880090-75-9
1. Magic—Norway—Elverum. 2. Manuscripts, Norwegian Facsimiles. I. Rustad, Mary S., 1952– . II. Title.
BF1622.N67S8313 1999
133.4'3'09481—dc21 99-30145
CIP

Galde Press, Inc.
PO Box 460
Lakeville, Minnesota 55044-0460

To the memory of

Oskar Garstein

Contents

Foreword

Mary Rustad has made a wonderful find. In a dusty old attic, she came upon two handwritten Black Books. In publishing them—and enlisting the help of Per Holck (a medical doctor and one of Norway's foremost authorities on folk medicine) to explicate them—she reveals a fascinating and important contribution to our understanding of a little known facet of the Norwegian heritage.

The Black Book—even today the name conjures up images of witchcraft and Satanism. Their terrifying reputation notwithstanding, they usually turn out to be practical handbooks for addressing daily concerns. They reward a modern reader by opening a window unto another age. The cures, advice, prayers, and incantations contained within their pages (and those to follow here) provide an intimate glimpse into the world of impoverished Norwegian peasants before the age of industrialization.

Magical Thinking

The books reveal not only these peasants' outward way of life—farming, fishing, hunting, waging war—but also give insights into their way of thinking where beliefs about witches, ghosts, and other manifestations of the supernatural firmly held sway. The Elverum Black Books speak to us from a time gone by, telling of the farmers' struggle for survival—their livestock threatened by wolves and bears, their buildings imperiled by fire, they themselves menaced by snakes and the fearful prospect of going to war. While finding tremendous consolation in their Christian faith, desperation drove many to seek protection in Black Book incantations such as those presented here.

Just as fishing and hunting augmented the meager food supply these farms could muster, the Black Books offer incantations to magically increase the yield derived from these activities: what if one could find a bottomless *huldrepond* teaming with unlimited fish or bewitch bullets to unfailingly seek their target?

On Norway's subsistence farms, butter was one of the few commodities whose production exceeded immediate nutritional need. It could therefore be used to pay taxes (old documents commonly express land values in measures of butter) and to barter for needed goods. Much could go wrong during the churning process, however, and rather than ascribing a poor yield to the cream's deficient butterfat content or improper temperature, they blamed it on envious witches or evil spirits, whose existence they did not doubt. Witches could cast a spell over the livestock, too. It therefore behooved one to discover who among the neighbors possessed such powers, and the Black Book provided incantations for this purpose as well.

The Elverum Black Books also reveal much about the cleanliness—or lack thereof—during pre-industrial times, when primitive facilities prevented all but occasional bathing, house cleaning, and clothes washing (all limited to about four times a year), while necessitating close contact with soil and soot as well as human and animal wastes. No wonder these pages abound with remedies for bedbugs, body lice, and infections. Equally strongly they reflect a fear of drifters and thievery; the peasants' impoverishment meant that lost property could likely never be replaced, even as the danger of theft constantly loomed and demanded recourse.

No recent phenomenon, the Black Books' formula for poking out the eye of a thief actually goes back to ancient Egypt, where it appears in the Magical Papyri, a compendium of remedies not unlike the Elverum Black Books. Many international incantations regarding personal health go back that far, too, and bear a remarkable resemblance to the cures printed here for boils, growths, fever, injuries, and excessive bleeding. Such afflictions would naturally befall workers whose bodies bore labor's brunt before the age of machines.

With the future of the farm depending on the next generation, Black Books showed special concern for women's reproductive health. We find incantations offering to enhance male potency, increase the odds of becoming pregnant, induce labor, ease the pain of childbirth, and encourage the flow of breast milk.

Nor does a reader look in vain for advice on abortion. While little stigma attended birth prior to marriage among courting couples, single mothers not only suffered intense social ostracism but also brought hardship among themselves, the child, and the community in this time of profoundly limited resources. Aiming to address psychological health as well as physical, some incantations sought to calm anger, cure alcoholism, or balance the prevailing hardship by instilling hopes of great wealth.

Magical Means

The actual materials and specific methods employed by the Elverum Black Books also speak volumes, not least of their users' desperation to find a remedy. With striking frequency they prescribe items associated with death (graveyard soil, a dead man's tooth), sin (deeds performed on Sunday when one should have been in church), or crime (a hangman's noose). According to international folk belief, these items join feces (or similarly putrid-smelling substances known as "devil's dreck"), bones, urine, and breast milk in lending extra power to accomplishing the words of the incantation. Evil spirits (thought to have caused the disorder) would find these items repulsive, so the thinking went, and therefore be warded off. Items associated with the Christian religion had a similar effect, so making the sign of the cross, reciting the Lord's Prayer, and singing a hymn also empowered these incantations, as did repeating the prescribed magical act three times and performing it on Thursday.

Though a few incantations do urge renouncing God and swearing allegiance to Lucifer, far more often they invoke Christ, St. Peter, the Virgin Mary, or the Trinity. Several of the Elverum Black Book's incantations employ the well known pattern from other Black Books of portraying one of these Christian figures suffering from, then ultimately prevailing over the same affliction the incantation aims to cure. Folklorists call the kind of wizardry that underlies such formulas "sympathetic magic." Resting on the concept that "like influences like," the idea was that the image of Christ or St. Peter overcoming the affliction would help the afflicted person overcome it as well.

The concept of like influences like also underlies formulas for curing fever or toothache that begin by writing a very long word, then repeatedly rewriting it, each time removing one letter, until only one letter remains. The fever or toothache, so the thinking goes, thereby also diminishes. In a largely illiterate society, words in themselves seemed magical, and this way of thinking also surfaces in the Black Books' instructions for making amulets by writing certain words on paper, which would protect their wearer from bullet wounds and other dangers.

By no means unique to Norway, the international pedigree of the means employed by these Black Book incantations reminds us that they have come down to us from ancient times, even as they incorporate elements from later cultures, such as the many Catholic prayers (and frequent use of Latin) and the Lutheran hymns. Nor did the Norwegians (or other immigrant groups) leave this lore behind when they came to America. Just such a Black Book, published in Chicago in 1892, enjoyed enormous popularity and is today found in the rare book room of Luther College's Preus Library. Who knows how many Black Books still may lurk in dusty old attics, also in America?

—Kathleen Stokker
Professor of Norwegian
Luther College
Decorah, Iowa

Preface

The publication of these two Black Books from Rustad in Elverum will turn out to be a major event in the study of folklore in the U.S. for various reasons. Americans of Norwegian descent will be given an opportunity to get acquainted with an intellectual universe unknown to many. In a wider perspective, these two Black Books may well serve as an excellent basis for the study of magic in general. It is to be remembered that magic is not a *mixtum compositum* of curiosa. On the contrary, magic has been throughout the centuries a means to survive various forms of hardships. The magical procedures present a certain outlook, a certain world view. Above all, it is a way of organizing life, a mode of orientation. Magic has to be studied in its various contexts. It is certainly dependent on these factors:

- The ecological system
- The historical background
- The social strata
- The frame of reference (the knowledge of tradition)
- The emotional attitude (hate, envy, expectations, eagerness, neighborly love, determinedness)
- Age
- Gender

- Profession (the knowledge of magic varies from one profession to another)
- The victim (whether the victim is a human being, an animal, or a supranormal being)
- Value
- The literary influence

Of course, not all forms of magic contain all these factors. There are nevertheless certain constant factors; namely, b,d, and j.

This shows that magic is never done in a social vacuum. By reading the charms and the recipes presented here, one understands that behind all these forms of magic there are certain resistant mental structures. With closer scrutiny, we will detect certain permanent patterns.

Many charms in this publication are to be found elsewhere in Europe and even in the U.S., brought there by immigrants.

The Black Books contain not only magical procedures, but medical recipes as well. They have served as medical handbooks in former times. They have been found not only at the farms in Norway, but at several vicarages as well! The clergymen used them when the cattle were attacked by more or less mysterious ailments or when people visited the local clergymen to seek advice for their illnesses. In former times, there were very few educated doctors in Norway. One had recourse to the clergymen or wise women or men well versed in the esoteric mysteries of magic. To cure illnesses by means of charms was considered legal because it was white magic, while using magic to hurt people was black magic. This is a distinction dating back to c. 1400. However, the authorities did not look at it that way. Many a wise man or woman was burned on the pyre in fifteenth-century in Norway for having practiced magic.

The contents of the Black Books presented here are very representative and fascinating. They give an insight into a world view now lost in industrial areas in our time but that may be detected in isolated enclaves both in the U.S. and in Europe.

One must be very grateful both to Mary S. Rustad and the publisher Galde Press for making these Black Books known to a wider reading public.

—Ronald Grambo
Former professor of folklore at the University of Oslo

An Old Dusty Attic

It is dark and dusty up in the old attic. Generations of spider-webs hang ghostly down from the rafters. Along the walls are old clothes, old family photographs, and torn feather blankets. Old boxes are everywhere. Over in a corner stands an old loom, seeming as if someone could have used it just the day before. The floorboards creak, but otherwise it is quiet.

Mary feels goose bumps, but she just loves to explore the old rooms on the farm. History is everywhere and it unfolds how people lived in the old days, especially women—what they had to carry, and what they had to be able to make. Women had a hard life, without a doubt. Many died in childbirth, others were worn out at an early age caring for animals and small children and because of sickness. There where wild animals and no cures for serious illnesses. Old letters have been found regarding sickness and death. It is thrilling to wander through history and be so near to her forefathers. Now and then Mary almost feels the presence of past generations. Are they near and looking over her shoulder? Maybe they are watching now.

Several of the boxes have been barely looked into in this century. Every box she opens reveals historical evidence of memories from times past: sorrows, loss, hope, love, and hate. Everywhere a living history of her kin.

Mary came to the farm, North Rustad, at the age of twenty-five in 1977. That year she married her third cousin, who was to inherit the farm. Her great grandfather was from the same farm and immigrated to America in 1879. Mary, of the fourth generation, has returned to her roots. All over the farm she can see traces of her great grandfather, his brothers and sister, parents, wives, and children. It is strange to think that after three generations in the United States, she would return here. It is both her husband's heritage and her own that she is surveying.

In one of the old boxes she finds two strange books. At first she thinks that she has found diaries, but quickly realizes that something is completely different. One of the books seems empty, but the middle pages are full of writing. It appears as if this script was meant to be kept a secret and is now long forgotten. She cannot help but notice that the pages in the middle are worn and have been used a good deal. After thumbing through the first blank pages, she comes to some pages that are handwritten in Old Norwegian and Gothic lettering. It is clear that not just anyone will be able to read what has been written here. The other book is bigger, with the title written on the cover. The pages are handsewn together. The paper is thick, almost like parchment. "A little book of skills," it says on the cover. All at once it hits Mary that she has found Black Books. They are Black Books! And there are two of them! In older times, a person could be punished for possessing occult literature. People were burned at the stake for the slightest suspicion of black magic or witchcraft. As a matter of fact, one of the last witches burned in Norway was one of Mary's ancestors.

Even if it was difficult to read what was written, Mary understood all the same that her discovery was a small historical sensation. This was a find that sent chills up the spine. The few words she could decipher revealed magic and incantations from a different time than the present. Nevertheless her curiosity was greater than her fear, and she took the books down from the attic. That first night, Mary dared not read the books while in bed. She walked around the house going through the incantations again and again trying to understand what could be written on these old pages.

Together with her husband she very slowly stumbled through several of the incantations. Some of them were scary, others almost comical. Counterclockwise, a swallow's heart, Belsebub: what does it all mean? Mary decides experts are needed to help with the interpretation of these books. An old friend of her husband was contacted and the books were translated word for word, later into modern Norwegian, then finally into English.

The books from Rustad are detailed compared to the other Norwegian Black Books and unique because every book is different. There are few remaining Black Books in Norway. Most were probably thrown away or maybe buried with their owner.

Fire could not destroy a Black Book. If the book was sold, the owner had to ask a price that was lower than what he had paid for it. It was important on the last point to follow the rules. (Remember just who you were dealing with here, a higher and a lower power!)

—Nils H. Rustad

Historical Introduction

The Black Plague that ravaged through Asia and Europe in the middle of the 1300s spread to Norway when a ship docked in Bergen in the year 1349. History tells us that one third of the population died because of the Black Death. Numerous farms were laid waste, and it took about 150 years before the population regained the same level as before the plague began.

Farms and small villages died out and were covered by forest. Decades later it was not uncommon for hunters and woodsmen to come across deserted buildings and farms in the middle of overgrown forests. One time a hunter, aiming at a wood grouse, missed the bird but heard a loud clanging noise where his arrow landed. He walked through the forest in the direction of the sound and found to his surprise that his arrow had hit the bell of an old, hidden church, all covered with trees. As he walked in the church and up toward the altar, he met a furious bear. The bear had wintered behind the altar. The hunter killed the bear with his spear, and the fur from the bear hung on the church wall many generations after this incident.

Little by little, life returned to normal, land was cleared, and people started farming the land again. In our part of Norway, Osterdalen (Eastern Valley), which is mainly known for its forest, a great deal of land was cleared in the middle of the 1500s, including the Rustad farm.

We know little about the time before the 1500s because of the Reformation, when most of the district's church books were burned. However, Rustad must have been an area where some Vikings lived, because artifacts were found in a burial mound in one of the fields just north of the present farmhouse. Objects, mostly weapons, can be seen in the National Museum of History in Oslo.

The name *Rustad* is a derivative of the Old Norwegian word *ruthrstadir,* or clearing place. Many of the farmers who lived on the farm took the name Rustad.

The first farmers, however, from the middle of the 1500s, did not live on the Rustad farm, which was at that time not a farm but was used as a forest pasture. Grass was harvested and then transported back to the main farm, in this case thirteen miles away. The first farmer on record is Bottolv Rustad in 1528. Bjorn Grundset started to use the farm in the 1500s. He was one of our forefathers, and died on Rustad in 1664.

Norway was unified with Denmark as far back as 1380 (Denmark-Norway). This union lasted until 1814. Much of the Norwegian culture during this period shows signs of Danish influence. Most of the governmental posts were filled by elite men from Denmark. They were here to protect the Danish king's interests. These men were officers of the crown. They were given large pieces of land, usually places where farms were few and far between. The Black Books found at Rustad could have been brought here by one of these high officials, or by a minister. Norway, at that time, did not have its own university. Norwegians had to study in Denmark in order to obtain degrees in higher education.

In 1709, Denmark-Norway was pulled into a Nordic war with the Swedish king, Karl XII. King Karl had lost large areas in Poland and Germany and wanted to take Norway as a replacement for what he had lost. The war lasted for twenty years and ended when King Karl was killed at Fredriksten Fort in Haldon, Norway, November 30, 1718. Rumors said he was murdered by one of his soldiers.

The 17th of May, 1814, was a very important date for Norway. Many influential men were chosen to participate in a meeting at Eidsvold. Ola Evenstad was one of 112 men who helped put together Norway's constitution. Ola was the brother of one of the author's forefathers, Helge Olsson Evenstad, born in 1777. Norway had only a few months of independence before the country had to enter into a new union with Sweden. The Danish king, Fredrik VI, who had been Napoleon's ally, had to cede Norway to Sweden. Napoleon lost after the battle of Leipzig in Germany.

Karl Johan, the Swedish king, was happy that Napoleon had been defeated. In the fall of 1814, the king sent forty thousand soldiers to Norway and forced the country into a new union with Sweden. The Norwegian people had to struggle for almost one hundred years before getting their final independence.

In November 1905, the new royal family of Norway came ashore in Kristiania (later called Oslo). The Danish prince Karl took the name Haakon VII, and ruled Norway as a good king until his son Olav took over in the 1950s. King Olav died in 1993. His son Harald is now the king of Norway. I have to add that the Norwegian people have always been very proud of their royal family.

Farm life on Rustad was not easy. The climate could be unfriendly, especially in the wintertime. At times there were floods and summer droughts. There was a big flood in 1789 when many of the farmers lost valuable farming land, as well as livestock and houses. It was after this flood that the Rustad farmhouses were moved farther away from the river.

Before 1850 the farming in Norway was more or less non-monetary. Everything was grown, made, and stored at the farm. In newer times, sugar and salt were bought by trading in hides and dairy products. Hunting was important, and traps (large holes) were made in the mountains, where moose, reindeer, and bears were caught.

In early times, the forest was used basically for firewood. Later there were sawmills along the creeks, and log buildings were replaced by plank buildings. Flax was grown and spun into linen, and clothing was made from cloth made on looms. Iron ore and blacksmiths played an important role on farms.

Most of the time there were fifteen to twenty-five people working on the Rustad farm. Some people were born there and many died there. The farm also served as a nursing home. When people became old, handicapped, or sick, they were taken care of and did not have to starve.

The potato was imported to Norway in 1750. Many ministers explained to their congregations on Sunday how to plant and care for potatoes and how to prepare them for eating. Around 1810 Norway had a hunger period, and the potato helped save the population from a major starvation catastrophe.

The Rustad farm went out of the family for several generations, but was bought back by Helge Tollefson Kilde in 1838. He was born in 1796 and was married to Ingebor Helgesdatter Melhagen, born in 1805. Helge bought the farm because his wife did not get along with his sisters who lived on the farm that he had inherited in Rena. Helge and Ingeborg had six children: Tollef, Helge, Gotmar, Johan, Ola, and Pernille. It is interesting to note that they were all scared of wolves, which were sometimes so hungry that they took farm dogs tied up by the farmhouse. The

Rustad farmhouse at that time was in a very poor condition. At night the children could see the stars between the logs in the wall. After breakfast, they had to participate in the tasks around the farm and everyone had to work hard.

The Black Books could have originated from one of two farms a little farther up north in the valley. Helge was from the farm. Kilde and Ingeborg came from the Melhagen farm. But this is only a guess. Both of these farms were large farms and the people who lived on these farms had the opportunities to come in contact with elite, educated people from Denmark, who would have had access to the Danish Cyprianus.

Editor's Note

I believe that my fellow Norwegian Americans will find this unfamiliar material about *Svartebøker* fascinating, just as I did. I do not in any way believe in or practice black magic. I also do not take any responsibility or recommend that individuals attempt to perform any of the incantations in this book. My only intention in putting together this volume is to enlighten Norwegian Americans about a portion of our history that has been swept under the carpet. Enjoy!

—Mary S. Rustad

The Black Books from Rustad in Norway

It must be considered a small, local, historical sensation that recently two Black Books have surfaced at North Rustad in Elverum, Norway, and that somewhere on the farm there is to be found a third one.

The farm of North Rustad has been in the same family since 1837, and it is not possible to confirm whether the books are from the farm's previous owners or were owned by the family before 1837. The family is from Kilde in Åmot and is a branch of the Alme family tree. Tollef Kilde can perhaps be suspected as the source of the books. He was born in 1772 and was father to the well known Tollef Kilde. It was Tollef's oldest son and first heir who settled down in Rustad. He could have taken the books as part of his inheritance from his father.

Nils H. Rustad remembers that many years ago he came across a Black Book with a black cover that has since vanished and is probably long gone. It was while rummaging through a number of old books and documents in the attic, and also looking for that first book, that Mary Rustad came across the other two Black Books.

The two books are both rich in content and are in good condition. One is a simple, pamphlet-like writing book with a gray cover, the type used in schools. The other is a thick, bound book with only some of the middle pages written on.

The two books are difficult to date accurately, but both the handwriting and content indicate that they are around the same age and from the period 1790 to 1820.

They also are in agreement with many of the other Black Books that are known from the same time period.

The books do not contain any names, initials, or dates that can help us to identify them. There are thirty-two incantations in one book and seventy-eight in the other. They are not numbered like many other Black Books.

Assistant Professor Per Sande of the public archives in Hamar interpreted and typed the books for the owner.

It is difficult to estimate how many Black Books there are to be found in Norway. Some of them are publicly owned by museums, in the public archives, and in teaching and research institutions, while others are privately owned. The number of books is probably between 100 and 150. There are a couple of private owners who own several books, but it is a rarity to find two or three books on the same property. Here in Elverum, we previously knew of only two other Black Books, one from Stenhammer and one from Findstad.

Svartebøka

Many have heard about *Svartebøka,* or the Black Book, but few have held one in their hands. The name alone gives many people chills up the back. I know one owner of such a book who dares not sleep in the room where it is kept. Not everyone can overlook completely that special texts or rituals can free dark powers.

One of the myths surrounding the Black Book was that it was written in blood, as a link in an agreement with the devil. But after the witch-burning era, this idea was toned down, and the books we know of from Norway were written with pen and ink.

In my youth there were many older people that denied or doubted the books' existence. This could be because people no longer believed in magic formulas, and the general opinion that no book could have such a subject matter could easily lead to the view that the book itself was a myth. The baby was thrown out with the bath water.

Because the book has a proper name, in the same way as the Bible, many believe that we are talking about a book with very specific contents and that one example is like another. But this is not the case. The books are handwritten, and scarcely two books are found that have the same content.

One major reason for the considerable differences is that most of the books originated in a period when word-of-mouth tale telling lived parallel with the written word. It happened that when a person got hold of an incantation, or several, or maybe a whole book, that person freely picked out incantations that seemed to be the most useful, not to mention current within the realm of local opinion, and slightly revised them with local and verbal tradition.

Another reason can be sloppy handwriting and worn-out books that have been difficult to decipher. Poor orthography and a lack of knowledge about alien words and foreign languages have led to writing errors and difficulties in making copies. It has especially caused problems when the foreign incantations were written in Greek and Latin and Hebrew. This is also a problem for today's Black Book interpreters.

Even if the result has been a number of individual books with clearly different contents, there are also books with similarities that clearly point to a common origin. One researcher will perhaps see a clear connection between them, but this is relatively uninteresting in a popular presentation of the material. It is however worth mentioning that two books respectively from Eiker and Jeløya have the most in common with the books from Rustad. However, there are only a few parallels with the other Black Books from the district.

Traditions with magic books are known from as far back as Babylon and Egypt. The Black Books' roots possibly come from Egypt, where in the first hundred years after the birth of Christ a number of books were written that represented mixed compilations of Egyptian and Greek philology, religion, and mythology, together with the Jewish cabala* and Christian superstition.

The tradition was further passed down by the scholars of the Middle Ages, who in the name of religion and philosophy were absorbed in classical magic. The study of the secret knowledge culminated in the 1500s and 1600s, the same time as the witch burnings. The Germans were industrious authors of magic literature, and many of the myths that surround the Black Book are built up around the theological faculty of the University of Wittenberg. Both magic books and the witch burnings found their way into Norway, where foreign and local traditions were blended together.

The book that has left the most impression on the Norwegian Black Book tradition is recognized as Danish. It is probably from 1608 and was written by a Lutheran minister and spread both in Denmark and Norway by the clergy. It was dedicated to the famous magician Cyprianus, who around the year 300 was the Bishop of Antioch and a Roman Catholic martyr and saint. Other known names that are associated with the book are Albertus Magnus, Paracelsus, Agrippa of Nettesheim, the German Dr. Faust, and

*The cabala is a system used by the Jews of the late Middle Ages in an endeavor to interpret and illuminate the Talmud. They were particularly interested in magical words and the numerical values of letters of the alphabet.

Pope Honorious. They are believed to be the authors of an incantation book called *Grimorium.* Many will also maintain that large portions of the magic incantations are taken from the Sixth and Seventh Books of Moses.

Some of the Black Books give indications about their origins without being necessarily reliable. In one of the books from Rustad, three claims are made:

> A little Book of Black arts/or a/summary of the/Cyprianus/that was written by Bishop/Johannes Sell from Oxford/in England/year 1682
>
> A copy of the actual Black book, written at the University of Wittenberg year 1529 and thereafter found at Copenhagen Castle in the year 1591 in a white marble chest, written on parchment.
>
> Remember that:
> These incantations that are found in the Cypriani Black Arts Book are sometimes so old that their sources are from heathendom, but for the most part they are from Catholic times. This can be recognized in the ancient northern ballads.

These three claims are a useful start for those who wish to find out more about where these two books from Rustad belong in a larger perspective.

The Black Book, in its early beginnings was used by few, if only because of the lack of reading abilities at that time. But after a while it had a larger circulation. It is assumed that, at the beginning of the 1800s, some hundred books were in circulation in Norway. They were used by people of widely different social status, from the clergy to wise people, who entirely or partly made a living by helping others.

Sickness flourished in the paths of undernourishment, uncleanliness, and unscientific reasoning. Skilled medical help was not to be found. Concerning medical questions, people therefore had to choose between the usual folk remedies that most people knew themselves or take the advice that could be gotten from someone who knew more than just the Lord's Prayer.

The following pages contain the complete incantations of the Black Books from Rustad. The contents vary from well meant and innocent folk remedies to the blackest devil conjuring.

The contents of the two books, like many other Black Books, is a fine blending of Norwegian and foreign folklore. One book is especially extensive and rich in contents.

The most extraordinary feature about these books is the almost total lack of advice concerning sicknesses caused by evil spirits, although Norwegian folklore is usually full of it. The explanation could be that the author lived at a time when the belief that sickness was caused by spirits was beginning to lose its hold. Belief in the other evil powers was clearly enough.

You are invited on an exciting walk through our forefathers' ways of thinking and living around two hundred years ago, in a domain that is written about very little in the history books.

—Ottar Evensen

End Liden Kunstbog

eller et

udtog af den

Sybrianus,

som var student af biskop

Johanes Sell i Oxford

udi Engeland.

A. o 1682.

A little Book of Black Arts
or a
summary of the
Cyprianus*
that was written by Bishop
Johannes Sell** from Oxford
in England
year 1682†

---

*A common name for black-art books.

**Bishop Sell was actually the English author, publisher, and clergyman, John Fell (1625–1686). Fell was the palace curator for Charles II and later headmaster at Christ Church College in Oxford. He became a bishop there in 1667. He published *Saint Cyprian,* which deals with the alleged originator of the Black Books, the mysterious Cyprianus of Antioch, who lived in Turkey in the fourth century. Cyprianus was a sorcerer and devil worshiper. He was able to free himself from the powers of demons and the devil by making the sign of the cross and converting to Christianity. Cyprianus became a bishop and was later honored as a martyr and saint in the Roman Catholic Church.

†This date varies somewhat in the Black Books that have been discovered previously.

Forerindring!

Disse Kunster findes Cypriani Kunstbog, er for det meste saa gamle, at
de har deres udspring fra Hedendom-
men, men dog meest i fra de Catolske
tider, som Landet var udi Kirkens
Bisperne. —

Motto:

Er du fornuftig. —

Naar et Creatur er befængt med
Lus eller andet utøy skal man tage
[illegible] [illegible] og stryge over Creaturet
en Søndag under Messetid naar Præsten
er paa Prædikestolen —

Remember that:

These incantations that are found in the Cypriani Black Arts book are sometimes so old that their source is from heathendom, but for the most part from Catholic times. This can be read about in the ancient Northern ballads.*

Motto:
If you are sensible...

When a domestic animal is infested with lice or other varmints, you should take warm ashes and spread them over the animal on a Sunday during the church service when the minister is in the pulpit delivering his sermon to the congregation.

---

*Northern Ballads: Ballads from the Middle Ages.

Et Copie af Den Ratte Sorte Künste Bog
skreven paa det Wittenbergske Academie Anno 1529
og siden funden paa det Kiöbenhavnske Slaat
Aar 1596 i en hvid marmor steen Kiste, og
skreven paa Pergament. —

Naar Du vil have udløst de afgrunds Engle da
skal du om morgenen naar du opstaar, sige saaledes: Jeg forsver dig gudfader som mig har skabt
[illegible] Jeg forsvære dig Søn Christus som mig igjen
løst. Jeg sver dig du Helli Aand som mig helligt
[illegible] vil til bede eller tiene Edes
[illegible] og aldrig
efter denne dag, og aldrig forsvære jeg ~~jeg~~ mig
under den afgrunds Høvding. Lucifer, og jeg
fører mig under hans Regemente, og hand skal
tiene mig og giöre hvad jeg af ham forlanger, og imod
jeg med mit egt blod til forsikring og under-
hand vil forpligte mig til ham med legeme og
Siel i all Evighed, der som hand giör det jeg
forlanger ham til = eller, hjelpe og betaler
og dertil segner jeg under min haand med
mit egt blod, og det er vist og sant i alle
Maader.

A copy of the actual Black Arts book, written at the University in Wittenberg,* year 1529, and thereafter found at Copenhagen Castle in the year 1591 in a white marble chest, and written on parchment.

When you want to release the angels from Hell, you should in the morning when you rise say this:

"I renounce you, God the Father that has made me. I renounce you, the Holy Spirit that has blessed me. I will never worship or serve you after this day, and I completely swear to Lucifer, ruler of the dark abyss. And I swear to his rule, and he shall serve me and do what I ask of him. In exchange I will give my own blood as insurance and a pledge. This insures me to him with body and soul for all eternity, if he does what I ask, order, or command of him. And thereupon I sign with my own hand and with my own blood. This to be certain and true in every possible way."

*The University of Wittenberg, Germany, is where the Reformation started.

B: 70

Den Dag du vil reise ud og Eder gider, skal du
opstaae i Diævelens Navn, paaklæde dig i Diævelens Navn, Ja! da skal ~~dig~~ Kimmer og ud-
gaae i Diævelens Navn, alt som du dig foreta-
ger skal skee i Diævelens Navn den Dag

No. 1

At mane de Onde Aander for at drive en
tyv hiem med det hand staalit. —
Jeg maner Eder i Diævle som haver magt at
binde saa vel paa Jorden som i Helvede. —
Jeg N: N: maner Eder i Diævle ved Himmel
og Jord, at i binde det menniske som haver
staalet fra N: N: atter maner jeg Eder i
Diævle at i ingen Rolig fred og Rile forunde
det menniske, hverken sovende eller vaagende Siddende eller liggende, gaaende eller staaende Ridende eller kiørende. —
Jeg lyser forbandelsen paa ham saaledes, at han
aldrig maa trives paa Jorden, forend hand baa-
ret hiem det hand staalit fra N: N: jeg besværger
og maner Eder i Onde Aander ved gud Fader
Søn og den Hellig Aand, og ved alle Elementer

Be aware of:
The day you will release and follow after Lucifer, you should rise in the Devil's name, get dressed in the Devil's name. Yes! Wash, comb your hair, and go out in the Devil's name. Everything that you undertake shall happen in the Devil's name that day.

No. 1

To conjure up the evil spirits to force a thief to return that which he has stolen

"I call for you, devils, that have powers on earth as well as in Hell, I [name] conjure you, devils, in heaven and on earth, that you stop that person who has stolen from [name]. Once again, I conjure you, devils, that you do not allow this person tranquillity or rest, neither sleeping nor waking, sitting nor lying, walking nor standing, riding nor driving. Thus I throw this curse on him, that he will never have rest on this earth before he has returned everything he has stolen from [name]. I beseech and call upon you, evil spirits, with God the Father, Son, and the Holy Spirit, along with all the elements...

at i aldrig lader dem føre nogen hvilken veed han bor, hvem det staalne godt. Abraham Isak og Jacob og Salomon skal binde dig D! den helige Korse som stod paa bierget Calvana, dergaa fri hvem var Spiget, det Lyspe Kinde Helena paa Sandt, og af hvitken Kors og Naglegrun bed giøre udkomne og et bidsel til sin Voss, rig maner Eder alle Dievle i Helvede, at i føre dette Menniske til bage med det han skaa lit svaldt og det med de vøßte Dievler som er nid Helvede og er

Asmodeum x Rickel x Belsebub x
Cordi x ~~Sailel~~ x Ferag x
Noranan x Belial x Diefael x
Raso x

Naar du da Land fornemme til nogen üroliged at det begynder at bulder og Riße i luften da du er nide paa fri mark, daar tegen til at de Onde Aander udevellot din befaling og vilder tegen

Hvorledes man skal binde de Onde Aander.
Naar du først har Manet dem üd, skal du trink 3 trin til bagr, og betegner dig med 3 Trei Korse et for dit hoved, 1 for dit bryst og 1 for dine fødder; og løser fader vor, strax naar du det gaaer

...that you never let that thief receive any rest before he returns home the stolen goods. Abraham, Isaac, and Jacob and Solomon shall help you. Oh! You holy cross that stood on the mountain of Calvary, on which the Saviour was nailed, that which was found again by the Empress Helena,* and from this cross and nail from the cross, she had made a crown and bit [for a horse] for her son. I call upon you, all the devils in Hell, that you lead this person back with everything he has stolen from [name]. With help from the worst devils that are in Hell, and they are

Asmodeum x	Richel x	Belsebub x
Cordi x	Jacbel x	Verug x
Noranan x	Belial x	Dicfael x
	Rafo x	

If you notice a disturbance where it begins to rumble and howl in the air when you are out on an open field, take this as a message that the evil spirits have carried out your command and are giving you a sign.

How to control the evil spirits

When you have first conjured up the evil spirits, go three steps backwards as you perform the sign of the cross three times on yourself: one for your head, one for your breast, and one for your feet. Then recite the Lord's Prayer. Immediately after you have done...

*According to legend, the holy cross was rediscovered in the fourth century by the Empress Helene, mother of the Emperor Constantine. The mass of the cross has since been celebrated on May 3.

giort, fra Sig skal rede: X Udi hvis navn disse Diævle ere udløst af helvede Udj Satans navn, skal de og fare dit i geen, for dig du og dine med brødre brød og i mod gud, og ville være ham lige, blev de for nedstødte i den afgrund, hvor du og dine skal blive, der for vil ieg bede gud at han ville stollige dette sted, som ieg staar paa, og ieg maner dig Lucifer med alt dit selskab, til dommer sted du kom i fra, og det i navn fader Søns, og den hellige aands Amen.

og siden den Psalme sjunges:

Vor gud han er ~~fra fasten~~ borg

At giøre sig haard.

tag en skale eller en steen i grevets hovede tag fra Liveden Jord og spore Sølv for 2 skilling og bær dette paa dig.

at Laste døren.

tag et Skale Øje og Last i drengen fra Lam den der i ligger udi de paa døren.

Kunst at see den som for giort en anden andens Kreature

tag Melck af en Nybdet Koe en Skee fuld Grevinde Melck en Skee fuld, af dit Egit vand en Skee

...this, say the following:
"I whose name has released these devils from Hell in Satan's name command that they shall be led back there again. Because you and your brothers did rebel against God and wanted to be his equal, you will therefore be sent downward to the abyss where you and yours will stay. I therefore pray to God that he will bless this place that I stand upon. I call upon you, Lucifer, with all your followers to return to the same place you came from. In the name of the Father, Son, and the Holy Spirit. Amen."
After, sing this hymn: "A mighty fortress is our God."*

To make yourself hard (strong)

Take a swallow.** There is a stone in its head. Take earth from a graveyard and two shillings worth of mercury and carry these ingredients with you.

To cause sleeplessness

Take the eye from a swallow and throw it in a bed so that whoever lies in it cannot sleep.

The art of seeing who has bewitched another's animals

Take a spoonful of milk from a cow that has recently calved, a spoonful of a woman's breast milk, and a spoonful of your own urine....

---

*This hymn was written by Martin Luther.
**It was thought that the stones inside a swallow's head could be used as a magic ingredient in medicine.

füld Blandt det tilsammen, Som det i et glas
og grav det ned i möddingen Kalten Over, og sig
3 gange disse Ord da du Setter det ned: Hosala
diesla Luga naar du tager det op saa sig 3 gan=
ger: nu gaar den som nu löb Belsebub i Hvide
admundus. — gaa ind i daglig stuen det
glasset paa bordet — 1 time derefter kommer
troldmanden eller troldqvinden, og begierer
enten Salt mad, eller og noget at drikke. —
men giv ham ikke men viis ham din vey naar
du iden vil hand skal gaa. —

at en skal Sove i 24 timer. —
tag galden af en kat, törre og stöd den til
pulver, giv ham den i Øl at drikke, sover han

at alle skal Sove i et huus. —
tag Øynene af et ugle hoved, leg det i vand det
ene flyder men det andet synker, tag det som
flyder, og en död mands tand, leg det over stue
döeren, saa skal folk at sove til lyst og tanden
er bort tagen. —

at ingen skal forgiöre dig. — skriv paa et stykke
papiir fölgende ord X Parto X amasias X Emanuel
X dorenus bær denne altid hos dig. —

...Blend them together. Put the mixture in a glass and bury it down in a manure heap overnight. Then say these words three times, while you are sitting down:

"Hosala Diesla Euga."

After retrieving the mixture, say this three times: "Go then he who now rules over Belsebub in his world." Then walk into the parlor and place the glass on the table. After one hour there will come a sorcerer or a witch and ask for either salty food or something to drink. But do not give it to him; only show him the way out when you want him to leave.

When you wish for someone to sleep twenty-four hours

Take the resin from a pine tree, dry and crush the resin to a powder. Then give it to the person you wish to sleep, in a glass of beer to drink. He will then sleep for twenty-four hours.

When everyone in a house shall sleep

Take the eyes from the head of an owl and lay them in water. One will float, but the other will sink. Take the one that floats and a dead man's tooth and hang them over the parlor door. The people in that house will then sleep until the eye and tooth are taken away.

Protection against being bewitched

Write on a piece of paper the following words:
"Porto Hamasias F Emanuel F dorenus."
Carry this with you, always.

at du ikke skal blive fangen i krig.

skriv disse ord paa et stöde papir, ff Lale ffalila ayrata b: b: d: f alias fff: bær denne steds paa dig.

At man ej skal skyde fugle.

tag et menneskes been, stöd det til pulver, bland det i krudet, er et forsögt stöder.

---

at skade vil ej skal skade dig

skriv disse ord paa et stöde papir: Araba Omel alifal Bultar iden et armoen Trola Boblamot Fasteanus. bær dette paa dig.

---

at hunde ej skal giöe ad dig.

bær enten hiertet eller öyet af en ulv hos dig, da ingen hund giör ad dig.

---

at vinde i handel, tag et Wibe Hoved og leg det i din pung hos dine penge, saa skal ingen bedrage dig.

---

at være skudfrie.

skriv paa et stöde papir fölgende ord: anel artus dun, bær skriften paa dig. om du tvivler kan du forsöge det paa en hund.

NB: det maa ligefald bindes til hundens örene

Protection against being captured in war

Write these words on a piece of paper,
"FF Lale FF alila ayrata b: b: U: F: alias FFF:".
Carry this always with you.

So you won't miss when shooting

Take a human bone, crush it to powder, and blend it in gunpowder. Use this blend of gunpowder in the gun. This is a mixture that has been well tested.

Protection from arrows

Write these words on a piece of paper:
"Araba Omel alifal Cuttar uden et armoen
Trola Coblamot Fasteanus."
Carry these words with you.

So that dogs won't bark at you

Carry either the heart or the eye of a wolf with you. No dog can bark at you then.

To win when trading

Take the head of a peewit (bird) and put it in your purse along with your money. No one will be able to deceive you.

To be bulletproof

Write on a piece of paper the following words: "Anel artus Dun." Keep this writing with you. If you have doubts about this working, try it on a dog first. But remember: the same words must be bound fast to the dog in order for the dog to be protected.

---

at gaae godt for at arbeyde hvad du paalagre dig. Skriv paa et stöcke papir med blod af en dödt hund, disse ord: max, pax, umax, Patris, filius, Spiritus Sancte. bær dennr seddel hos dig, saa skal det gaae got for dig. –

At Döve Skud.
naar du hörer et Skud saa tag og en torve under din höyre fod, vend den om og leg gröngsværen ned, saa længe torven ligger saa, kand bössen ey gaae løss. –

at ulve og biörne ikke skal skade Kreaturerne.
tag ulve og biörne been, stöt dem smaa, og giv dine Kreature i forsæt en torsdags Morgen. –

at Döve Ormer Edder.
Jesus og St. Peder gik sin vey, fandt en Mödder de en död mand, hvad skader dig sagde Jesus? han Jorn Klingelmand har stunget mig, stak og du skal faae bod i samme stund i 3 navne, fader vor 3 gange. –

At stille skarp Ild eller vaad Ild eller Vandne. De Egg som bliver lagte om skiertorsdag kaadene aldrig, 3 af dem som bliver kastet over en skarp Ild i 3 navn slucker den strax. –

To free yourself from promises you've unwisely made

Write on a piece of paper with the blood of a black dog these words: "Max, phax, umax, Patris, Filius, Spiritus, Sancte."* Carry this paper with you. Then those unwanted promises you've unwisely made will vanish.

To avoid bullets

When you hear gunfire, pull up the sod under your right foot. Turn it and lay the green side down. As long as the sod lies this way, guns cannot fire at you.

So that wolves and bears cannot hurt cattle

Take the bones of a wolf and bear, crush them into small pieces. Give this salted to the cattle on a Thursday morning.

To weaken the poison from a snake

"Jesus and St. Peter walked down a road. There they met a dead man. 'What has killed you?' Jesus said. 'Jon Klingelmann** has stabbed me,' replied the dead man. Jesus said, 'Stand up and you shall be healed instantly.' In the name of the Holy Trinity." Recite the Lord's Prayer three times.

To put out a flame or an accidental fire

The eggs from a chicken that are laid on a Maundy Thursday never rot. Throw three of these special eggs over the fire. Do this in the name of the Holy Trinity. The blaze will be put out immediately.

*This distorted "Father, Son, and Holy Spirit" seems to be taken from Catholic liturgy, which can help contribute to dating the incantation.
**Jon Klingelmann is an old nickname given to a snake.

Paa anden Maade. —

Skriv følgende ord paa et stöcke Blyg og kast det Over Ilden. Ordene ere: Anoram, Emanran, Natan. NB: Prøv med en Steen af samme Slags som Blyet om du kand naar Over Ilden, for om du ikke kand kaste Over Ilde branden med Blyet kand du kommer i ulæyenhed. —

At bort skriue Colla

Dette skrives paa et stöcke bröd og gives Patienten i 8te dage, nemlig: 1 Stöcke i hver dag, og den 9de dag, og brendes det sidste stöcke som er, C X.

Colameris x, ~~Colamerx~~, Colamer x, Colame x
Colam x, Cola x, Col x, Co x, C x -----

Om Kort og Terninge Spil. —

Skriv disse ord med et nyt blod i din haand, Rør ved Kortene der med, skal du vinde. — Ordene ere: Nasi Akis Porus. —

At vinde i Rettergang. —

Tag en Ørne tunge, haf den hos dig i 3 Søndagers Masser i Kirken, bær den siden paa dig. —

Another way to put out a fire

Write the following words on a piece of lead and throw the lead on the fire. The words are: "Anoeam, Emanean, Natan."
Note: Try first with a stone that weighs the same as the lead to see if you are able to throw it on the fire, because if you are not able to throw the lead on the fire, you may find yourself in trouble.

To cure a fever (colla)*

Write this on a piece of bread and give it to the patient for eight days, specifically a piece each day, and on the ninth day, burn the last piece, which is C x.
Colameris x, Colameri x, Colamer x, Colame x, Colam x, Cola x, Col x, Co x, C x
After doing this, the fever will be gone.

To win at card and dice games

Write these words on your hand with your own blood. Take the cards in your hand. You will then win.
The words are: "Næsi axus Porus."

To win in judicial proceedings

Remove the tongue of an eagle and take it with you to church three Sundays in your side pocket.

Nasi axus Porus

*Colla or cold-fever was a name given to all fever sicknesses that began with the chills.

Jtem.

först skal du om Morgenen for en Sorlen gaar og og, gaar for din Naboes Döer, meden leder Klud, den du da skytter ud 3 gange, og sig: Nome Astarolt. naar du saa kommer for Detten, holder du Kluden i din höjre haand, med tommelfingeren i Haanden indföjet, da du tver verdelig paa din Naboe, saa siger du disse ord ved dig selv: Jeg seer dig med 6 öjne, 2 mine 2 dine, og 2 fanden; du skal tie og skal tale, Luciførs fanke skal binde dine hender og mund, dig til skade og mig til gavn i Nassa Augusta Deel Regneon og Mortosication Hadrok Segena Amen.

at fiske i alle vand.

Saar lin de fordom kring vandet, siden faar du fisk i Mangde Wiis.

at løse Blomma fra öjet.

Jesus og St. Peder gik vejen frem, der möte de en blind Mand, Manden sagde, giör mig mine öjne gade, som din Moder gord, du hendes öjne giorde gord, i 3 Navn, saa fader vor.

Ditto

The first thing in the morning, before the sun rises, go to your enemy's door with a small rag. Spit on it three times, and say: "Nome Astaeoht."
When you stand before the court, hold the rag in your right hand with your thumb bent inward. While looking righteously at your enemy, say these words to yourself:

"I see you with six eyes. My two, your two, and the Devil's two.
You shall be silent, I shall speak. Lucifer's chains shall bind your hands and mouth. You shall have the disadvantage and I shall have the advantage. In the name of Augusta Deck Regsition and Mortification Hadrok Segena Amen."

To fish in a hulder's pond*

Sprinkle the dirt from a graveyard around in the water. After that you will catch fish in quantities.

To heal an eye infection

"Jesus and St Peter walked down a road, there they met a blind man. The man said: 'Make my eyes as well as your good mother; you made her eyes well.' In the name of the Holy Trinity." Then say the Lord's Prayer.

*A hulder was a wicked fairy. She was very beautiful, but she had a tail. People thought that a hulder had a pond with a double bottom where there were particularly large quantities of fish.

at stille Værck.
tag en Kråke, tag hende hendes hierte og steit
det paa en hinde, tag saa tungen af Kragen
og leg den under din tunge, og les saa og Kråke
hiertet, naar saa noget er værck paa dig saa leg
den tunge under din tunge og tale med ham,
stiller hans Værck.

---

at vinde i Rettergang.
Naar du har en Kråke tunge under din tunge
da du Prosenterer vinder du.

Om Kraake stener.
det siges at en Kraake har 3 stener i sin Rede
dem skal man tage en torsdags aften
efter at Solen er neder, den ene er hvid, den
anden sort og den tredie Rød. den hvide stene
at bære paa dig, bliver man aldrig Sörigful-
den Sorte at bære befrier en fra at icke bliver bedragen af noget qvindfolk, og for den
faldende Syge. den Røde at bære, befrier fra
Tyverie, og at haver den i Munden da man
kysser en pige, da elsker hun dig over maade.

To calm anger

Take the heart from a swallow and spear it on a stick. Then take the tongue of the swallow and place it under your tongue. Then display the swallow's heart. When someone is angry at you, display the swallow's heart, then place the bird's tongue under your tongue and speak to him. His anger will stop.

To win in court

When you are attending judicial proceedings, place a swallow's tongue under your tongue. The case will go in your favor.

The magic from swallow stones

It is said that a swallow has three stones in its nest. The stones should be collected on a Thursday night after the sun has gone down. One is white, the other black, and the third red. Carry the white stone with you and you'll never have sorrows; carry the black and you will never be free from not* being deceived by any woman or the falling sickness.** Carry the red one and you are saved from being haunted by ghosts. And by having the red stone in your mouth when you kiss a girl, will make her love you in every way.

---

*The word "not" must not be omitted here.

**Falling sickness is epilepsy.

at giöre dig usynlig

Stick Hjernen ud paa en flagre Muus og forvar har dig, og smör dig over med flagre Muus blod, tag saa Hjert af en sort Kat, bag det i söd Melk, ed og drick detter saa er du usynlig i 9 timer.

---

at en skal sove i 9 dage.

tag törret Hare lever, stöd den og gived hud i brendevin og Ell Adike, og lög Hare lungen under hans hoved, saa sover hand til han faar Ell Adike i munden.

Kunst at bekomme og have lykke til Penge. slaa saa den Hemligen af en sort Kat, giör dig deraf en Pung, den förste penge du derefter faar skal du styge Mynten af, lög den Hemligen paa en lig grav lad den ligge der i 3 torsdags Netter, tag den saa igien, og da faar du Pöt et under, lög den i den Pung og lad den aldrig komme der af igien. siden skal du hver Höytids aften, som er Juul, Paaske og Pinse aften, kaste en Skilling bort lige i Nord, og sige: denne faar giever jeg dig du gudgiverske Dalilt. siden Mangler aldrig Penge.

To make yourself invisible

Poke out the eyes of a bat and put them in your pocket. Smear yourself with bat's blood. Then take the eye of a black cat. Cook it in sweet milk. After eating and drinking this, you'll be invisible for nine hours.

To sleep for nine days

Take the liver from a hare that has been dried, crush it, and serve it together with alcohol and sour beer.* Lay the hare's lung under the person's head. That person will then sleep for nine days or until the sour beer mixture is poured in his mouth.

The skill of receiving and having luck with money

Skin a black cat in secret. Make a purse from the hide. The first coin you get thereafter must be rubbed against the purse. Secretly lay the purse on a grave and let it lie there three Thursday evenings. Retrieve the purse again and you will see a wonder. Place the coin in your purse and never take it out of there again. Hereafter, before every holiday evening (that is, Christmas, Easter, and Pentecost Sunday), you must throw a skilling** toward the north and say: "This gift I give you, you the goddess Dalix." You will never lack for money after that.

---

*In old days the over-yeasted beer was badly preserved and could easily sour.
**A skilling is a copper coin formerly used in Norway.

At binde Nedsadt gods. —

I Jesu navn! dette gods som her ligger lönligen og er af Mennesker Nedsadt, det binder jeg med 3 band som er 3 navn, Ja! jeg forklarer det med guds ord men jeg tvinger og formaner eder i 8te Helvedes Förster, som er: Lucifer, Belsebub, Astarott, Satanas, Anubis, Drytiannus, Drakius og Belial, at i med al eders Sælskab viger herfra, og lader dette gods komme i Menneskers hænder. — her med truer jeg dreyer med min söd Jesus! som er guds og Marie Sön, hielpe mig bot og styrke mit mod, at annamme dette gods i det hellige velsignede guds navn, Nu vil jeg det annamme med min Hand. i 3 Navn saa Fader vor. —

At vise Igien en tyv. —

dersom du vil vide hvem som har staalit, da tag Rögelse og Saaske tyv eller mercian, viet vand, og melk af en qvinde som haver födt drenge börn, af dette giörres en Confæckt, tag saa en Speegel og smör glasset over med denne smörrelse, skriven som aftenen en torsdag

To protect hidden goods

"In Jesus' name! These goods that lie here concealed and that are hidden by people, I claim them with three bands that have three names: the Father, Son, and the Holy Spirit. Yes! I have the power with the word of God. I compel and exhort you, Hell's eight princes, who are: Lucifer, Belsebub, Astaroht, Satanas, Anubes, Dryttianus, Drakeus, Belial, that you depart from here with all your company. Let these goods come into human hands. After saying this, I stamp my foot. Jesus! who is God's and Mary's son. I strengthen my courage to take these goods in the holy and blessed name of God. I now take these goods with my hand, in the holy and blessed name of God. In the name of the Holy Trinity." Then say the Lord's Prayer.

To point out a thief

If you want to know who has stolen from you, take incense and Easter candles or marjoram, holy water,* and breast milk from a woman who has delivered a boy child. Make a dough out of these ingredients. Then take a mirror and smear the glass completely with this mixture at 9:00 on a Thursday evening.

---

*This is obviously from Catholic Church services and can contribute to dating this incantation.

og skriv et hierte midt i Speeglet, ~~...~~ og disse ord om kring, saaledes som følgende Figur udviser. –

Jesu Christi Hierte og i Hierte,	Eli. Eli. Eli. Eli. ♡ Lama Asabthani.	Eloi i gjennem tungen med Skjødet –

Gjöm siden Speglet i et mörkt Rum i 3 Nætter, gaa saa til Speglet igien, saa skal du der paa finde tyvens navn og hvor han igien findes. –

At Sikkre en Tyv.

Skriv følgende ord over Dörren der tyven har staalit, saa kommer han igien: – – –

Auratabul – Auratabu – Auratab –
Aurata – Aurat – Aura – Aur – Au – A –
og disse ord skrives 9 ganger. –

En formaning at løse i Dalk og Rindende Vand for at give et menneske som er kast Ondt paa, eller er forgiort, og det skal skee en torsdags aften. – I dag, som er d: N: N: dag over den ganske Christenhed, løser jeg ved guds kraft og Magt og ved Jesu Christi Finger, der nogen forgiørelse er giort af troldqvinder, af Fugle eller fiske bein, af Norden eller af Sönden. –

Draw a heart in the middle of the mirror and write these words around it, as the following figure shows:

Jesus Christ's side and heart

were pierced through with a spear.

This done, hide the mirror in a dark room for three nights. Then go to the mirror again and you will then find the thief's name and where he can be found.

To put a spell on a thief

Write the following words over the door of the house which the thief has burgled.

Auratabul—Auratabu—Auratab—Aurata—Aurat—Aura—Aur—Au—A

Write these words three times. The thief will come back again and can be caught.

A spell to be read over salt and running water

This to is to be given to a person upon whom evil has been cast, or who has been bewitched. Perform this incantation on a Thursday evening:

"Today which is D.N.N.* day over all Christendom, I read these words with God's power and might and with Jesus Christ's finger. I point to wherever bewitching has been performed by witches, using bird or fish bones, by the north or the south...

---

*D.N.N.—the Lord's.

Vind, af Jord, eller af Bierge eller Söe Trold,
af nogen Gienfærd eller Ulÿcke af inden eller gaaer
i Mad eller i Drikke, Sovende eller Vaagende,
gaaende eller staaende, Siddende eller liggende, sti-
dende eller agende; da binder jeg i Dag deres
Been og Lunger, deres Hierter og Tunger, deres
Hænder og Födder, og deres forbandede Hierte Rödder
de skal under Stöder og Steene og aldrig mere
giörre Menniske nogen Meenne, ved den Höyeste
Kraft og Magt i de 3 Navn skal de vige fra
saa som Salt for det Rindende Vand, Amen,
læs Fader Vor 3 gange.

at læse bort Værk.
Jesus gand ved over Broen den bratte, der
grentede Steen paa gaagers den Svarte Jesus
steg af, og lagde sig selv ned og bötte, Værk
bort, og kommer igien i sorten Mölle, og
Ved i Ved, og Been i 3 Navn, læs Fader Vor
til Ende.

for den flyende Græsa.
Vor Hr. Jesus og St. Peder og St. Andreas med
de andre Disiple, de gik op med Aaen og ned
med Aaen, der mötte de den Slemme Græsen,
der kom op af Vandet som en Fisk og

...wind, by soil or by mountain or water sprite, on purpose or by accident, in or outside, in food or in drink, sitting or lying, riding or driving. I hold today your liver and lungs, your heart and tongue, your hands and feet and your cursed heart's roots. You shall never do more harm to any person. I say this with the highest power and might in the name of the Trinity. You shall remit yourself to these words as salt for the running water. Amen." Then the Lord's Prayer three times.

To heal an injury*

"Jesus rode over a steep bridge. There waiting on the path were the evil dark spirits. Jesus walked by the evil spirits and knelt down and healed an injury. The leg and foot bones met again, and joint met joint again. This being performed in the name of the Trinity." Then recite the Lord's Prayer to the end.

For airborne epidemic infections**

"Our Lord Jesus and St. Peter and St. Andrew, along with the other disciples, walked up and down along the river. There they met a terrible being that came up out of the water as a fish and...

---

*"Injury" here means all kinds of joint and bone injuries (sprains, breaks, etc.)
**People thought epidemic infections were due to arrows shot by the evil powers.

wille opsluge dem, Jesus greeb henne i Kjolen, og sagde i hvor skal du hen? hexen sagde: jeg skal i N. N. gaard, at der fordærve baade Hester, Sviin, qvæg og faar ~ brende Bygd, Hiärtet Ade, Blodet drikke ~ Nej! skal du icke, sagde Jesus! du skal i girund wende, til du dig udsender, i Aaen i gjerne, og i det størster Dyb der gaar. ~ J 3 Navn. ~ fader vor 3 gange.

Mod trold qvinden. ~ Kloms Bönne.

Jesus og Jomfru Maria gik over broen den bede, der mötte de troldqvinden leede, hvor skal du hen sagde Jesus? jeg skal i bondens gaard, og der fordærve Menneskers qvæg og faar, Høsten og foer, i Nirende leed. ~ Nej sagde Jesus! du skal ned, du skal komme dod, over dennen bed, fra du skal gjennem, i Jordens Röder, og i den forbandede Söder, i 3 Navn, og siig 3 gange fader vor. ~ dette kaldes og:- [star] .-

Kloms Bönne .-

Om Hund eller wil bide gaaet Creatur eller et Wilt Dyr eller en wil Fugel, som undertiden gaar Efter til.

Denne Konst er Efter Kyllig, og bestaar der i: =

...tried to swallow them up. Jesus grabbed it by the tail and asked: 'Where shall you go?' The evil spirit answered: 'I shall go to [name] farm to harm horses, swine, goats, and sheep. There bones to break, meat to eat, and blood to drink.' 'No! you shall not,' Jesus said. 'You shall turn back to them who have let you out, down in the river again, and to the greatest depth there is.' In the name of the Three."
Then recite Lord's Prayer three times.

A prayer for protection against witches

"Jesus and the Virgin Mary walked over a wide bridge. There they met the witch, Lede.* 'Where are you going?' Jesus asked. 'I'm going to a farm and injure people, goats and sheep, horses and cattle to the ninth generation.' 'No,' Jesus said, 'you shall go away, you horrible bag, over this brook. You shall burst in the very roots of your heart and in your cursed feet.' In the name of the Trinity." And then three times the Lord's Prayer. This is called a "protection prayer." ⛤

If you are having trouble shooting accurately at wild birds or animals

This trick, which is often used, consists of...

---

*Lede—the evil one.

at man skider Lovs i Kuglen eller i Haglen
eller man kan tage Brende stene af ildsta-
den i Kidgnet, eller nu den stods paa La-
minen, leg det i geværet og skyd saa Dyret
der med.

---

at forware Dig i Kirken paa Höijtiders Nætter,
da man vil see trold Kelfer.
Det er en gammel Sigen at i 4re Nætter i Aa-
ret faar troldqvinder Magt at wise Sig i Kirken
Nemlig: om Jule, Paaske, Pinse, og om Söndags Natten. naar du wil see dem, skal du
om aftenen gaae ind i Kirken, eller og kan
du staa uden for, og have i fölge med dig Be-
wergield dyvelstræk, korn og malt, og blade
af en gammel Kirke psalme bog: du skal
med en Lidz giöre en Ring om kring dig,
og i det samme du træder Ringen lang-
somt, siig: Jeg Jesu Navn saa staar jeg
her, i Navn faders og Söns, og den hellig Aands
amen. Da man staar udi denne Ring til Proces-
sen er forbie over Klokken 12. — om nogen
taler til dig, enten det følge, eller nogen af
det andet følge, naar du ikke giver Svar,

...cutting a cross on the bullet or on the gun. You can also take hot stones from the fireplace in the kitchen, or from a fireplace anywhere, and put them in the gun. Then shoot at the animal with it.

If you wish to see witches

There are old tales that state, four nights a year, witches have the power to appear in the church; namely, at Christmas, Easter, Pentecost, and on the Midsummer's night. It is possible to see witches walk around in a church in the evening. Stand outside a church and have with you castoreum,* dyvelsdrek,** grain and malt, and a page from an old church book. Make a ring around you with a stick, and at the same time you draw the ring slowly around, say: "In Jesus' name I stand here, in the name of the Father, Son, and the Holy Spirit, Amen." After 12 midnight, stand in the ring until the process has been finished. If anyone talks to you, either from one group or anyone from another group, do not answer....

---

*Castoreum is a bitter, strong-smelling, creamy, orange-brown substance that consists of dried perineal glands from the beaver and their secretion.

**A strong-smelling substance, *dyvelsdrek,* devil's dirt. It is from a plant that people thought would hold the evil power at a distance.

NB man kan og staae ved Kodrene, da det
er tilforladeligt at de kommer der, da de
gnager nogen materie af dem med tenderne.

Et andet:
Hud det skien allene en Jordtorre og paa Kirke
gaarden, om det er paa saadan Aares tid, da
de legge den paa hovedet, da de staae hvor de
vil, udenfor eller inde i Kirken, uden at have
nogen andre ting med sig, og ikke i Ringen,
men at staae i Döbe Funten er det bedste
middel i Kirken, der som det er saadanne
Fontus.

Den saa kaldte fisker Bön.
Jesus han paa landet stod, bad en Petter om
en Nod, Petter giorde som han sagde, Noden
ud i vandet lagde, Jesus sagde: fisker Nod,
nu skal du faa, udaf storr udaf linaa Fiske
Jeg nu og fange vil, for mig noed hör fisker
til, med Guds kraft, med Guds Magt, I 3 Navn
fra Fader vor til Ende.

Om en tyv legger dit skarn efter sig, da den
han Stukit.
Tag glorende Ildmörge og dække den deraf

…Note: You can also stand by the church bells, since it is very likely that witches can be observed there because they like to gnaw on the bells with their teeth.

Another way for protection while observing witches

Cut a clump of sod from a church yard, but only if it is in the right season. You'll be able to stand where you wish if the sod clump is placed on your head. You can stand inside or outside the church. You need have no other protection with you, and you don't need to stand in the ring. But standing by a baptismal font is the best protection in the church, if the church has such a font.

The fishing prayer

"Jesus, standing on land, asked Peter to find a boat. Peter did what he was asked. The boat was out on the water. Jesus said: 'Enough fish you shall now catch, of big and small size. I catch and will catch plenty of fish sent with the help of God's power, with God's might. In the name of the Trinity.'" Then say the Lord's Prayer to the end.

If a thief leaves his turd behind him after he has carried out a burglary

Take glowing live embers and sift them over…

den lagde Baren, med Disse Ord: Saaden giører jeg dig, for du staalit fra mig.

Et Andet

tag Barnet, som er saaledes lagt, stag den i en Hammel Gieders Pibe, tag gæst eller gang og sæt til at den Baren æser eller færmenterer udi nogle Dage, leg saa yderst Piben i Elden med den ene ende, Jo meer du vil Pine tyven, Jo Varmere Land du lade piben bliver, Ja lige til tyven styrter, men hvor dog livet. naar du legger piben i Ilden, saa Sig samme Ord som i første post er mældet.

Sud Rude eller Ørgestiden at giøre samt Omtalte sted. Ruden skal skiæres paa langfredagen og paa paaske dagen, himmelfarts dagen, pinsedagen og paa St. Hans dag, alt førend Solen gaar op. Stæderne hvor med dingen giøres skal skiæres i 2de Söndags Morgener paa Nyt, alt med nye Kniver som aldrig har været i brug førend da.

…the turd which was made, while saying these words: “The Devil I send to you, because you have stolen from me.”

Another one

Take the turd that has been left behind. Stuff it in an old musket pipe. Take yeast or sourdough and place the turd in an environment so the mixture rises and ferments some days. Then place one end of the musket pipe in the fire. Yes, the more you wish to torture the thief, the longer you can let the pipe lie there, only ’til the thief falls, but spare however his life. When you lay the pipe in the fire, say the same words that are stated in the first part. (“The Devil I send to you, because you have stolen from me.”)

To make a divining rod

The mentioned stick: the divining rod must be cut on Good Friday, Easter Sunday, Ascension Day, Whitsunday, and on Midsummer’s day, and always before the sun comes up. The stick must be cut anew on two Sunday mornings, always with new knives that have never been used before.

Rudens Besværing.

Jeg N: N: besværger dig du edle Rude i Navn G: F:
og den Hellig Aands, at du sandferdeligen viser
mig, klaar og fører mig an paa det sted paa
hvilken er guld, sølv, eller penge, som er
af menniskens hænder giort, og ere forwarede i
og under Jorden, og det saa vist som Jomfrue
Maria var en Reen Jomfrue, for og efter føde
selen, saa vist og sandt som Christus er Guds Søn
og saa vist og sandt som Guds Søn døde for Men-
nesckens Synder, og er alle Menniskers Frelser
jeg besvær dig Rude med den Magt og Kraft
hvormed Jesus Overwandt Dievelen og alle
Onde Aander, og giort dig den underdanig, jeg
besvær dig, at du allene slaar ud paa gamle
skatter, som er af Menniskene nedsatte, og icke
paa Nogen anden Ertz eller Metaller, eller Nogen
anden Ting, og allene bliver ved det du Nu er
befaldet, og det for hele Naturens skyld, som
det guddomelige Wesen bestyrer, ved Guds hellige Evangelium, Hans Hellige Ord, ved Engler-
ne, Martyrerne, Dievlenes fald og fengsel, og
ved den store Basune lyd, som paa Dommens dag
skal giøre liv i alle døde Naturens levende.

Swearing over a divining rod

"I, [name], beseech you, noble stick, in the name of the Father, the Son, and the Holy Spirit, that you truthfully show me, point out, and guide me to the place where there is gold, silver, or money, which has been made by human hands and is hidden in the earth. Be as true as the Virgin Mary was a pure virgin, before and after the birth of Christ.* So certain and true as Christ is the son of God, and so certain and true as God's son died for man's sins and is all mankind's savior. I beseech you, stick, with your might and power as Jesus conquered the Devil and all evil spirits and made them most humble. I beseech you, stick, that you alone point out old treasures which are hidden by man, and not any other minerals or metals. Continue looking when you are commanded. With God's holy gospel, His holy word, with the angels, the martyrs, the Devil's downfall and confinement, and with the loud trumpet's sound that on the day of judgment shall give life to all natures dead and living...

*The incantation is obviously from the Middle Ages.

Skabninger som har været til paa Jorden i
og saa vist og sandt som Himmel og Jord skal
forgaae med Ild, og en Dom følge, ligesaa vist
og sandt skal du Odde Rune ubortalst Ret an-
vise for mig de nemte ting, og det i de 3 Navne
Amen.

at giöre dig Død.
Da skriv disse Ord som følger og bær dem paa
dig: Tetgar: Tattrim Tebra Saleombia I:O:T:H:

at du aldrig skal skyde feil
tag Svovligen en Staal Krog af et Fruentim-
mers Klæder, det er best men saa kand man
ved sige at nøyagtig [illegible] Lægger, disse Lægger
man en udal i forladningen i Geværet eller
mellem Krudt og Hagelen, da man siden skal
ey skyde feilt paa Dyr eller fugl, men ikke
at skyde til maals med.

at giöre blæk som er ferdig i 24 timer.
Man lader til den fin de galæble koge med skie
vand, og kommer der paa vitriol, tillige med
lidt Gummi Arabicum, og Salmiak, saa faar
man et blæk som forsvinder af Papiret efter
24 timers forlöb.

...creatures that have been on the earth. And so certain and true is this that like heaven and earth shall perish with fire, and that a judgment follows, equally so certain and true that you divine, genuine stick, and shall show me the treasures I have named." And all this must be recited in the name of the Trinity. Amen.

To make yourself horny

Write the following words and carry them with you: "Fetgar: Fættrim Fobra Jahcomhia. J. O: F: H:"

So that you never will shoot incorrectly

Take in secret a steel hook from a woman's clothes. They are best, but you can well use hooks that have not been used. Place the hook on the outermost part of the muzzle-loader of the weapon, or between the powder and the shot. After doing this, you should never have problems shooting correctly at animals or birds. But never shoot at targets when using hooks.

To make ink which only lasts for twenty-four hours

Let a gall nut* cook together with nitric acid until the solution is dark in color, then add iron sulfate together with a little gum arabic and ammonia. This mixture makes an ink that disappears from paper after twenty-four hours time.

---

*Gall nut—a swelling of plant tissue usually due to fungi or insect parasites and forming a source of tannin.

at fordrive et Foster.
eller at give en Pige ind, at hun skal
blive quit din Byrde, om det er ei
over 5 Maaneder. Det skal drives
Vand viis af den [illegible] svor. blaaeste
Farver er farvet, til det en nogle gange
er den forsøgt.

Et Andet
Med god Brændevin givet Lam og drives Fostre
bort fra Fold. og Fæ.

Et Andet
Safran med en Dram fransk Brændevin
drives og stødt.

---

at et Skiød skal taste følt.
lad hende lugte paa forste Svine Tarme

---

at drive Mol Drue af Livet paa en
Qvinde eller en Koe.
Vaske [illegible] med Brændevin 1 eller 2 gange
Livet.

To expel a fetus or to give to a girl so that she can be rid of her burden, if it is in the first five months*

She should drink cups of this soup wherein a blue stone color** is cast. Drinking of it several times, she will then abort.

Another one

Strong castoreum can also expel a fetus from people and cattle.

Another one

Saffron mixed in a drink of French alcohol forces strongly.

So that a mare shall give birth to its foal

Let the mare smell fresh swine intestines.

To force milk from the udder of a cow or a woman

Wash the udder/breast with alcohol once or twice.

---

*Even today an abortion after three months is estimated as risky.
**Copper sulfate—very dangerous!

at en Kue, skal gaae giøm om
Sommeren af sig Selv til Tyrallen.
tag Salt i en Klud kast det 3 gange
mellem Dørerne og Broggen med disse
Ord. In° Domini Deus Patria
et Spiritus Sanctus Amen.

at Døsen skud
skud! staar stille for guds skyld! som skabt
Himmel og Jord, og den gandske Verden
for Guds Søn, og for Jesu Christi
lidelse skyld. Amen.
NB: bind disse Ord paa Brystet

at en Pige skal elske dig og følge dig.
Skriv disse Ord paa et Eggee og giv
hende nogen skage wid, Bell, Pelom
, Corocersii.

at en Vandrer skal giøre af at drikke
brendeviin. tag 3 Mand Negle log
dem i brendeviin i 14 dage i Skiul lad Patien-
=ten

So that cows will come home during the summer by themselves at night

Take salt in a rag. Pass it three times between the chemise undergarment and the naked body while saying these words: "Inn Domini Deus Patria et Spiritus Sanctus Amen."

(It is understood here that the cows are given the salt to eat. The salt has the scent of the woman who takes care of them. The cows should easily now find their way back to their caretaker.)

To endure a bullet

"Bullet, stand still for His sake, for He that created heaven and earth and the entire world: By his judgment and Jesus Christ's sufferings sake: Amen." Note: Bind these words to the breast.

So that a girl shall love you and follow you

Write these words on a cup and serve her any kind of drink: "Bell, Pelom, Corocerstu:"

So that a drinker shall give up drinking alcohol

Take three baby mice: Lay them in half a pint of alcohol for fourteen days. Let the patient...

Driv der ud Detto. —

Vægge Lüus at fordrive. —
tag en Fliis af et Nagel det som du
i Vægge Sprænger ... der udløget er ska=
[illegible] det. —

at en [illegible] Landsforderwe til [illegible]
Bondegield, [illegible] [illegible]
[illegible] [illegible] det at [illegible]. —

at et Menneske som er forgiort af
Kierlighed, kan blive god igien —
du skal hemmeligen tage eller Kliper Haar
af hans eller hendes Hoved, og lege det i
din venstre Skoe en tiid og gaa der paa
saa brænd det paa Ovnen. —

at Luus [illegible] skal [illegible] paa dig. —
tag et Menneske Been paa Kirke gaarden
og Som det ind i dine Klæder men tag [illegible]
[illegible] paa en Sÿke Brakedage. —

...drink it up.

To drive away bedbugs

Take a sliver from a wheel (torture instrument) and set it in the wall crack where the bugs are. The bugs will soon be gone.

So that a girl can expel her fetus

Castoreum, devil drink, put in alcohol to drink.

For a person to feel normal again after being bewitched into love

In secret, take or clip hair from his or her head. Put the hair in your left shoe and walk on it for a time. The unnatural, bewitched feeling usually goes away.

So that lice shall not thrive on you

Take a human bone from a graveyard and sew it into your clothes, but don't take the bone on Tycho Brahe days.*

---

*Especially unlucky or dangerous days named by the Danish astronomer Tycho Brahe (1546–1601), who calculated such days for the Holy Roman Empeor Rudolf II of Prague.

~~at hun aldrig skal drives paa dig~~

at drive Foster fra folk. — Tag Sevenbom
Tag den kogt og giv Patienten det at drikke
paa fastende Mave. — Probatum. —

at en Hoppe som bruges at lade bespringe sig,
og dog ej bliver frugtsommelig. —
Vil du at hun skal blive frugtsommelig og du
under gaaende det, saa du uformerket og med
Næven fra Haand 3 slag bag over Skeden
under Dig eller Hovet, hvorunder Øjnene er
blevne i skiul slagen end. — Probatum. —

Om du er udenlands og vil vide om dine
Frændinger og Skyldfolk ere døde. —
Vokke skal Du om Sommeren og da opkaster en
liden Sten som ligger i Jorden der ingen Stene
er! Under den Sten du den skal kalde de Augne
Mark; er den Munter og frisk, betyder at den
Slegt er frisk, er den ganske mager eller betyd-
der at der er nogen i din Slegt som er mager
syg eller udfattig, døer den allene for vaade-
vært Kiun efter Maaneden eller Madiden
...

To expel a fetus from a woman

Gather juniper berries and cook them immediately and give this to the patient to drink on a empty stomach. Probatum.*

For a girl who usually has intercourse and is not with child

If you want your woman to be pregnant and you allow her that, nonchalantly and jokingly hit her three times on the back of the skirt using a stick or cane with which a worm has been beaten to death. Probatum.*

If you are out of the country and you want to know if your relatives and kinsfolk are dead

This can only be performed in the summer. Dig up a little stone that lies in the earth where no other stone is. Under the stone you will see a worm. If it is lively and healthy, it means that your relatives are well. If the worm is powerless, it means that there is someone in your family sick or incoherent. If you only see decayed mucus from the worm,...

---

*Probatum—Proven. Means that the spell has been tried successfully.

det betyder at du ske noget sendre faa og ligge dig paa Hiertet i din Slægt er død.

at skaffe et Menneske bestandig Hovedpine — allene at du kan faae nogle Hovedhaar af hans Hovedt og sætte det i en trang Kløft udi en Træe hvorudi med Kilen an, den naar vinden kløfter med disse Ord: Hovedverk i Fandens Navn

for den som skal gaa Skiedstad.
Taa Egge Hvide og Salg eller Smelte som man og Rygge ... sammen og stryge ind mod Ilden 2 a 3 gange —

at bøde Vored for din Hiorn i Krig læs disse Ord: Wor Herre han drag i Herrens Færd Han bøde alle Swagers Værd, alle Swagers Værd han skal den tag Hans Odd og Eggen fra at de ikke skade han hverken Qvinde eller Mand Petrus med dit Sværd giorde en Fandens Færd, i 3 Navn. Fader vor. —

at giøre en skiemt Coffe god igien — giør den noget varm ved Ilden og gisk den med Older skiis saa længe du vil igien. den som skiemte Bossen.

…it means that the person in your family you think most about in your heart is dead.

To cause a person a constant headache

Get some hair from his head and fasten it in a tight crevice where two trees rub against each other when the wind blows and say these words: "Headless in the Devil's name."

For a man who is going to run the gauntlet*

Take raw egg whites and suet. Melt this together and smear the man's back with it and have him step in toward the fire two or three times. (The suet will then stick firmly to the back, adding protection against the blows from the whips.)

To dull the sword of your enemy in war

Read these words: "Our Lord, He went on a gentleman's expedition. He dulled all the drawn swords. 'All drawn swords,' he said, 'I take from them point and edge, so they cannot injure, neither woman nor man.' Peter with his sword did the Devil's mischief. In the name of the three." Then recite the Lord's Prayer.

To make a jinxed gun perform correctly again

Warm up the gun by a fire and whip the gun with alder twigs. Continue whipping the gun as long as you wish to torture him who has put the hex on your gun.

---

*Gauntlet—To run the gauntlet was a military punishment where a man had to walk between two lines of a whole company of soliders outfitted with whips. Each man was allowed one blow to the man's back.

Et Andet. — [illegible] 3 gange dag
[illegible] giver om at [illegible] Blodet [illegible]

at Binde Ormen —

Orme Dören [illegible] skal staaende til ren
fald nu O! Orm jeg binder dig med Guds
ord saa kraftelig, at du ligge skal for mig
fri, jeg igien løser dig, Christus og en
[illegible] Haand, de Haand [illegible] der for den
stand at du [illegible] skal Gaa, i 3 Navn
fader [illegible]. —

At [illegible] at man der [illegible]
[illegible] Hornene om det ude er [illegible]
[illegible] Skilling. NB. [illegible] han er
[illegible] [illegible]. —

Om et Menniske [illegible] eller fader
[illegible] om [illegible] gaarden eller det
[illegible] i [illegible] i [illegible] Kisten
til [illegible] er man [illegible] gaa [illegible] Menniske
[illegible] gaar igien. —

at [illegible] og [illegible] gaa fold [illegible]
ud med [illegible]. [illegible] den med Vitriole
=olie. —

Another one

Pull her three times backward through a freshly split roan tree. (It is difficult to determine what this incantation was meant to help.)

To stop a snake

"Woman the seed shall thread, snake the seed in until fall. I command! Snake, I stop you, with God's words so powerful, that you shall lie paralyzed for me until I release you again. With Christ's and Paul's hand, freeze! You cannot injure! In the name of the Trinity." Then say the Lord's Prayer.

When your churning won't make butter

Throw a piece of silver into the butter churn, even if it's nothing but a silver two shilling. Observe: Silver has a strong binding power.

If a person haunts after death

Spread linseeds around the farm where the deceased once lived. His ghost will then go away. You can likewise spread linseeds in the coffin with the deceased. You are to be assured that person won't haunt again.

That boils and growths on people break out fast

Coat the boils or growths with iron sulfate.

END OF BOOK ONE

Lucifer.

Anu skal giøres Saar
Dan slaab Eg gierne for Dit
Stiaag —

Tagen Skalla Arg nu ned fra
i Hundes Hanund i tag Dau
Ginid [illegible] meile Res-
Gregsolt [illegible] Dagleg idelau
Mnesfor arnd Hulk Vaadn
eller Saaned i 24 dimier

Sved Breev

Sose mando aasilutas Sabra Speii
sera hapat tabenta Sesa Sanan
Of vadua elamas pulmorum
Famaselse sajsas Brema asfuit
debmus Saara seeras lovalo
Servato Cabi Lolulos in Nomi:
:ne Matris Sieuis spiritus amen
Sag Samen Under Kaad Elaig

In order for a man to make himself hard as steel, like iron from an axe or knife. First take the stone from a swallow's head.* Then take white soil from a graveyard and one halfpenny's worth of mercury. Put the fixings under your left armpit. You will be strong for twenty-four hours.

An Incantation.

"Sole mando oasiluta Sabra Spesis
Fera habat Tabenta Jasa Sanar
qvadua dimas pulmoruno
famaseise Sapas Crema alfunt
debmus Seara Seraslos alo
Seurata Cabi Lolulos in Nomi-
ne Matris Sieuts Spiritus Amen.**
Keep this written incantation with you....

---

*It was thought the stones inside a swallow's head could be used as a magic ingredient and medicine.

**This incomprehensible and meaningless incantation contains distorted fragments from the Latin liturgy. The medical advice probably dates back to the Middle Ages.

Paa bjerder altvig ont Saadaig
Brobtunnet

at haa aller til at
Maaue int Lius

Sagt Forbladet eda Skrain
Salmen ord yaa sagley
Ein under Dopfodenn
Elo Elläm Fagian
Grantem

Aabenbareen
Lijs

[illegible] Diissen ord yaadt
Ikker af [illegible] Otlum Vand
[illegible] Vaa haden Vor 3 Söndager
Saforude Yaa efter [illegible]
[illegible] aiuend naar Yaud Kom
[illegible] Vaud [illegible]
til Vaa [illegible] Yaud efter ret

...This incantation can be recited for protection against being attacked.

Probatum est.*

To make everyone in a house dance

Take an aspen leaf and write the following words on it: "Elo Elleam Fagiam Grantem." Then lay the leaf under the doorstep.

To reveal a thief

Write these words on a piece of cheese with alun** water. Then read the Lord's Prayer three Sundays over the cheese while fasting, never saying Amen. Have the person that you believe to be the thief eat the cheese....

*Probatum est—It is proven.
**A solution of mineral salts.

[illegible] for Haand Skjeldag

+ Tag en [illegible] Vaa brydes Haand

Ord Krage og Ignaudare:

:nur [illegible] [illegible] Onaxpax

Firax Juller Strax elips

Ord Haa [illegible] vregibea

Exgriedo Avaro Tentr

am Tuam Tasie Dollore

Paa en anden maade
at Vinne [illegible] det som
han har Saalet +

+ Tag en gloende Maandags
Morgen [illegible] ~~Haand
Haand~~ [illegible] [illegible]
[illegible] [illegible] som
[illegible] [illegible] [illegible] [illegible]
Haand og sig dem 5 gange
+ Hasel. agel tor Hasel: [illegible]
længe som [illegible] —

...If he is guilty of thievery, he will immediately throw up. The words are these; "Max, Pax, Firax." Or write these words on the cheese: "Neguba, Exgvieda arraro Finte am Tuam Tasie dollore."*

Another way to get back what a thief has stolen

On a Monday morning, take hot embers and lay them in a mustard-seed grinder and turn the grinder counterclockwise** with your left hand and say these words five times.
"Hafel. Ageltor. Hafel."
It won't take longer...

---

*This incomprehensible and meaningless incantation contains distorted fragments from Latin liturgy.
**Counterclockwise—to move against nature was an important principle in the art of magic.

gjenn gaar advent den
kring med den gladlinge
saa skal og det menniske
som haver staalet fra
N:N: gaa til baage
igjen til mig og linge
som denne glad bren:
:der saa skal og det
menniskes hiarte brendes
og aldrig ud slukes
för nu han ber hiem
igjen det N: som han
har staalet & tag saa
glöden af gjennemigjen
og trod under dem.
höjmen stod og sig saa
skal skal slut hiarte

...than turning the grinder with the embers counterclockwise before the thief who has stolen from you will give the goods back to you. And as the embers burn, so will that person's heart burn and never stop burning before he brings back again the goods that he has stolen. Then take the burning embers and step on them with your right foot, and say: "Like this ember shall your heart...

blivr Vam Imm
glad Vam Imr glad
Vam Imm glad i under
min fod i nafn
faders Vön og helig
aands Ord B forstaae
er beskrevet 3 gange

Paa en anden maade
at Komme en Tijv til
Bage.

Tag nu fuldting i den
Haand og gak sål ftl Vand
Vam Kunden hva Vönden
og tål navn og det nu
Sønsdags aften og Vaij
Vaaing Manerdag skal
og naaanee at i ikke
Kunne Kaa Imntijs

...be. Just like this ember under my foot. "In the name of the Father, and the Son, and the Holy Spirit." Read this incantation three times.

Another way to make a thief come back

Take a coin in your hand and go to where water is running from south to north, on a Thursday night, and say this: "I command you, sun and moon, that you do not shine on this thief....

Jeg maaner dig Lüsiffer
med alt dit Selskab x
O! jeg maaner dig Fanden
og Helvede x: i staa paa
Pindingen i Sandet
at i ikke gjøre denne Syg
Hjørnen Smalle eller
Kor Hornn Sand bortal
ringe gjenn dit Dam
Hærne Baalet hva N.N.
Gud lade denne Sijn ikke:
faa nogen gadlagnnmnt
Smale eller Kor Dag eller
Nat morgen eller
aften slaad Sanis Hjerte
brenden dannen glod
der ikke [illegible]

...I call upon you, Lucifer and all your followers. And I conjure the Devil from Hell." (Then throw the coin into the water.) "Do not give this thief either rest, relaxation, or tranquillity before he brings back to me that which he has stolen from me. God do not let this thief have any rest or tranquillity, day or night, morning or evening. Let his heart burn like a burning ember that can never be extinguished....

og lad Ham blæ[illegible] urolig
Som en Vand bølge paa
den Vilde Strandbrede
for den Sijn til bage vend
Ent N: Hand har Staalet
fra N: N: til det [illegible]
og las Som det udtaget
Hannes tilkommen og
Sker i Sancti Divles Navne
Samt i Helvedes afgrund
Sändnig og [illegible] den
de 10 Helvedes Skjødsler
Som til [illegible] antegnet

...And let him be as restless as a wave on a wild beach, until he has returned the goods he has stolen from me, to the spot or place it was taken from.

This shall fully happen in the Devil's dreaded name that lives in Hell's abyss." The names of Hell's ten princes can be added here.

---

at slaa Öjet ud
paa en Tyv—

Tag Peter af en Sönnavegen:
Alm og Mand blad fra
Söndags Morgen under
midsommer blande det til
Vannen at det bliver Van-
ne dog skriv paa Öjet
der under saa borte
og slaa Sand om kring
paa under paa stölgen —

~~Hudt~~

Diabolus [symbol] Agstart

No.

Tag Vaa en Svaber
Vagnt Vanne Vnidt
en Söndags morgen

To put out the eye of a thief

Take the fat from a chicken and mercury and man's blood, on a Sunday morning during the church service. Blend together to make a dough.Then draw an eye with this mixture on a table with these words around it, as follows:

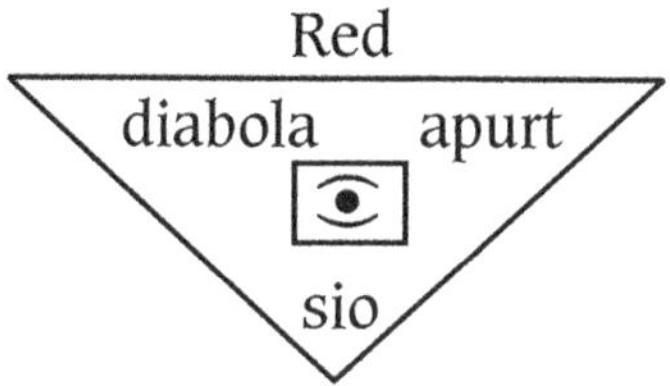

Then take a copper nail that has been forged on a Sunday morning...

før du kan gaa i 3 slag
under dem i divelens
navn; sodt saa naglen
faa ørgent og slaa 3 slag
und dem hammer
og sig; Satan Beelsebuse
Bellial: Asftarathaller
ladeln dem i hølvede

at seeen Tyvi vand

Skriv stålgande ord
paa et skiln saaydes
Siembra fiat Tasit Nameum
Pempsis alfigvidm Tinut &
lig det under en bordfas
paa i 3 Sorskelags udsen
tag det saa i hånd og
Slaug Blegmidt saa
hen andre sinde

...before the sun goes up, made with three blows from a hammer in the Devil's name. Then set the nail against the drawn eye and strike three blows with the same hammer and say: "Satan, Beelsebub, Bellial, Ashtarath, and all the devils that are in Hell."

To identify a thief in water

Write the following words on a piece of paper:
"Siesnbra fiat Tacit Nameium Dempus alligeum Tinut."
Let it lie under a heavy stone three Thursday nights. Pick it up again and spread bleach water on the other side...

og Lund skriften og det
det staaë i en skaal med
det 4 Söverer med Hvid
Jomfru Vagx skjeld paa
skaalen med brand paa
Kan Alt Pen tiënne paa
Nyt i 3 timer brend
paa og figuret —

Om Kierlighed med
Quinder —

Tag et kruger öl og
Hvid pigen sål
skiænk Vinden fult
i egen taßt paa et stöl
Svale blad eller i englad
finder Quäbler

...then turn the written side up. Fasten the paper to a plate with white virgin beeswax* on the four corners. Then fill the saucer with water and you will then see the thief's face for three hours. Then burn the image.

How to awaken love in a woman

Take a cup of beer, and give her a toast. Then fill the cup again, adding a little swallow's blood, and let her drink...

*Virgin beeswax was sold at the druggist under the name *Cera alba.* Virgin beeswax was really only wax from young beehives, and the wax had a dirty white color.

Paa Hor Dyn dag
Hurtelig alder

Ditto at

gak tilnu Vaalekarde
og tag denu Vaale, dag
alle med bor Hand tag

At Hille Blod

Det Var nu Helligsie dag
stund at Jesus Lams
Marie sund Hand Løse
af fra den Kriger Blod
Paa Helig nu med dit

...After drinking this she will be very loving.

Ditto one

Go to a swallow's nest and take a swallow—never with bare hands, however— and take...*

To stop bleeding

"It was a blessed time and period that Jesus was in Mary's embrace. He rose up so beautifully from eternal death with his...

*The original text stops here.

blod vaa Röd og vaa
Vinsfælig Som det er Van:
:dt og Aift vaa Biller
Detter blod Ved Jesu Chri:
:stes magt og i Jesu navn
amen ; i nominare
fader : Son

At Stille Skade
Ild eller Varme

Skriv disse Ord paa
Dørren i det Huus Som
ilden giör Skade og Skri-
Dørren ind og giör det
bat sammen Da udslukes
Ilden ; [illegible] disse
4 Erbum die Manet
Me Terunem

...blood so red. And to be sure that this is true and certain, stop this bleeding in the name of Jesus Christ and his power.
Amen, minonare
Our Father."

To stop a damaging fire

Write these words on the door of the house that is burning and break the door down and make it silent. The fire will extinguish itself. The words are these:

"I Erbum die Manet
Me Terunem."

At stille Blod Flod

Vat stiller blod flod paa
N: N: Sign Dam Brön:
:nen stillen stod der
Jesus i med dine 10
Disiple over flod i Jordans flod:

Ditto at

Vaet stiller blod paa
N: N: Sign Dam den
grümme Satan ud i Hel:
:vede ~~[illegible]~~ Saa staa Jesu
Har Himmen fanget og
bunden i Helvede Der
Skal han staa —

To calm a flow of blood

"Be still the bleeding of [name], like the current stood still where Jesus and his ten disciples crossed over. In the name of the Trinity: The Father, Son, and the Holy Spirit."

Ditto

"Stand still the blood of [name], like the terrible Satan in Hell that stands steadfast. Jesus has trapped and bound him, in the name of Three [the Father, Son, and the Holy Spirit]." Then recite the Lord's Prayer.

For Tanverk

Skrif þessi ord á hreint Bök-
papir legg þau þá á 13 Bök-
lad þau liggja undir þann
fyrsta hjá þann andr-
Tönd um aftaninn og
um morguninn Bölstuur
er liggur þau á Polden
og lögnludur undir
andur tör Morguninn
Aftan ordinum eiðr
Agerin Nagerin Vagerin
Pagerin Spagerin Sibia-
Detta skal skrifast und
nu nijr yeur —

For a toothache

Write these words on a piece of paper. Then cut it into three pieces. Have the sick person place the first piece on the bad tooth in the evening and, in the morning, quietly spit the paper on the fire. Do the same morning and night with the other pieces. The words are these:

"Agerin Nagerin Vagerin
Jagerin Ipagrin Sipia."

These words should be written with a new pen.

Ditto et

Skriv disse ord paa en
Vindel Baan skal ingen
paa det Bord man har
ondt i Aanden

Ageroni Pegerom Negerom
Pipia — det ord Pipia
Læses for Tunden

Ditto paa Gamle

Denne Skrift
skal fortæres
i Velograg den
det slag
og bindes
det Vipse Dan
nr 1 R* xxx
iii:

Ratalibus x / Ratal x
Ratalibu x / Rata x
Ratalib x / Rat x
Ratali x / Ra x
R* x
N.B. xxx iii:

Ditto

Write the following words on paper money. Then place it on the bad tooth.
"Ageron, Jegerom Negerom Sipia." The word "Sipia" is thrown to a dog.

Ditto

Ratalibus x
Ratalibu x
Ratalib x
Ratali x
Ratal x
Rata x
Rat x
Ra x
R xx
NB: xxx iii

This writing shall be conducted in the course of 8 days, and on 9th day burn the last which is left.

Rxx xxx
iii

[This incantation is for a toothache. Like the previous incantation, these words are written on paper. Start the first day with the word Ratalibus x and place the paper on the bad tooth. Then every day thereafter, write one less letter. This is continued for eight days. On the ninth day, burn the letter R xx. The understanding was that, as the word got smaller, so would the pain.]

Om Kortsag
og Terning Spil

Den Som nogen Dan
Har giort Sig et Bond
af en Bøkre af et Kruke
Som er Slagen Hengt
i og Bind Om Landliner:
Ter Som Ola Vinde
ingen ifra Slag —

Ditto

Tag blod af en Sort Hund
og Skriv disse Ord
vax pax dax —
da vinder ingen af
dig

Regarding card and dice games

If you are able to make yourself a band from a piece of a noose with which a thief was hanged, no one will be able to beat you at the game you are playing. The band has to be tied around your left arm.

Ditto

No one will be able to beat you at cards if you take blood from a black dog and write these words:
"Rat, Pat, Cat."

Ditto at

toy Zürtut aßne
mülevarpse
ëuidr[illegible] eläu [illegible]
arm[illegible]l ela[illegible]
[illegible] at [illegible]
[illegible] ag[illegible]
[illegible] Naun [illegible]
b[illegible] [illegible]
[illegible] katigle

Ditto at

[illegible] [illegible]
[illegible] [illegible]
[illegible] af nu Flangen
[illegible] ag [illegible]

Ditto

Place the heart of a mole under your left armpit.You'll then have luck when playing dice or cards. The same can also be done with the heart of a wood owl.

Ditto

Take either the heart of a black male cat or the heart of a bat and sew the heart in...

gnävnig. Vilte-Klud
og hav lägnende uti
Olat Menißen annehit
og Sigehar hav Vaa
Vagter Vind dag Vsly
naar du skal spile
gin Vinder i spilet
sund dag i ßnam

Detto at

Tunggslinshrör og
Dinor Det i Nogy
og hav det [illegible] ad
Dag Vaa Vinder
den

...a new, green piece of silk. Place it in your left armpit. Then say quietly to yourself when you're gambling: "I'll win the game against you, in the name of the Trinity."

Ditto

Take salamander eggs and mix them with wax and keep the mixture on your person. Then you will win.

Dittent

Hvaÿ clängr Or Dreund
~~Lait~~ clät nyndrle lae
i clain Sänd Nesi
Axlis Poriis

at Fiitre Diïnd
Fuiglenllin Diïn

Längsr clid gaandid
af clain clar clogak
baglnndir ay Diÿ.
Minati agunar clii
Haunr iil flangnie
cla Lay Z Slijbn Tord
Tunclaud c~~laim flood~~
clain Bruflur flod
ogslah Oapnr claigi

Ditto

Write these words on your hand with your own blood: "Nesi, Axus, Porus."

To make birds or animals stand still*

When you first step out of your door, walk backward and say: "Minate." When you reach a forest, take three pinches of earth under your left foot and cast the...

---

*To hinder or restrain an animal and make it stand still so that it can be killed.

Corps 3 gange og Sig
før 3 me gang Hall-
gal Saa 3 gange
baglunds i min Kiste
ymod Soelen og Sig
Saa før Me gang X.
naar du ver flegler
eller dijr da [illegible] paa
munde dine Kiegler
og Sig Saa x Otte maat
vaat [illegible] der mange
dijr da skud Saa
mange du Vil [illegible]
Som 3 lad dem gaae
der 3 dijr da skud de
2 lad det Belin gaa

…dust three times and say each time: “Hall.” Then walk three steps backward in a circle counterclockwise and say this for each step. When you see birds or animals, point at them with your finger and say this: “O AXMAX VAX.” If there are many animals, shoot as many you want, but spare three. Let them go. If there are three animals, shoot two and let the third one go….

ve dag at døje den skiønhen
da tog den Snaag og
skiære et lincket Bokken
Gidd inden den
Bruystor Armstad
Lagt det i Nord og Sig
x habe Mihi x Vignrofamp
ve den Stugler daskijden
da Ukri det Bruysten
ben af og Lagt bant
under daugge ved
Sellama Zallua —
mirk Vindelen den
Sanne om Sahmen der
i ne Retr bandt agden
Vindel Skal Sunge

...After shooting an animal, take your knife and cut a little piece of meat from under the left front leg. Throw the piece of meat toward the north* and say: "Habe mihi siger lamp." If it is a bird you shoot, twist the left foot off and throw it away while saying "Sellama Lallua." Write on a piece of paper. The paper must be straight and hang...

---

*This must be interpreted as an offering to the evil powers, which live in the direction of north.

i sin Mød Pilter Fraa
Om den Hals, Dein
følger ———

1772

Hr. Fry N: N:mann
og Herr Seig Ole gud
Baron Neric L. Ashflarht
at i alle tail Finder Rengst*
eller Tiugel Kalben Penninger
Wänger til Pinder-flor
assaidt Skind, matz
Ordber Oth. as: max

R. G. E. F. R. nt
C. m. E. E.

...on a red silk thread around your neck, with the following written on it—

4 7 3C I [name] conjure and swear to you the god Naron Neriot Ashtart. No animal or birds can run, leap, or move to one side of my bullet. But I kill it in the name of ax max
23 I T F L n Ts
m 3 7

Af Fietrgen
Hans Löben

Hagen Blud af Hans
[illegible]
[illegible]
[illegible]
[illegible]
[illegible]
[illegible]
[illegible]
og gak ud paa
[illegible]
[illegible]
[illegible]

To stop a drifter

Take a piece of the drifter's clothes, even if it's no more than one thread. Place it in the middle of a grindstone and turn it around three times counterclockwise. Then take the thread again and go out on a field and throw it toward the north as far as you can. Throw it up toward the sun at sunrise, and say...

Vaad 3 gange, Vaad Sam-
men han igien Om
han Haver bond Vadt
Prob: x Och clæderne
Før meig efter mungt
siz bage der hvem
Slued eller Traad
Har dreit i clæderne
i navn i Faderens navn
i Sønnens navn —

...this three times. Then he'll come again as if he were confused.
Probatum: "Oh you Devil before me, return this person who owns this rag or thread, in the Devil's name, in the Devil's name, in the Devil's name."

At en Piege
Skal Elske dig

Der skrives at Nafnen
skal han 3 Gange i
Din Vand Krol Röd
Vort og 1 Graad Da skal
tager Din anden Tiine
om torsdagen efter
Solennes ned gaart
Din Röde at Ligge i Kin
nemmed og Siffrene
gange da har Hun
dig Saitr Gierne.—

For a girl to love you

It is written that a swallow has three stones in its nest: one red, one black, and one white.* The stones should be collected two hours after the sun goes down on a Thursday. Put the red stone in your mouth when you kiss a girl, and she'll then take you as her sweetheart....

---

*It was thought that the stones inside a swallow's head could be used as a magic ingredient in medicine.

Din Vorte at bære
for Kovne clü aldräig
af nogen grænd Folk
og dagen clü og hvær
for falden Byjgne
Din Hände at bære
blässe clü aldräig
Porge fuld i nogen
maade

...If you carry the black one, you will never be seduced by any woman, and you'll also be free from the falling sickness.* Carry the white stone, and you'll never be sad in any way.

---

*Falling sickness: epilepsy.

at Ulve og Biörne ikke skal
tage eller Creatur At Vaar.—

Nu Lukker ieg mine Creature i
Dag frem paa den Grönne vol,
Som Jomfru Maria Dijrbare
Sön. Taiernis Bödöel stadt og
Seiermand. tag nöglen i haand
tils for Ulve og Biörne og
Trolkiering haand. for alt det
som mine Creature skad-
kan. . . Terrilla.
i Jesu navn Gud Fader Sön og
heligaand. og læs paa Naden
Vaar.—

Dette skal læses udi Valt og ind
giönne den udi Valt og indgiönne
den Paskmich, Om Nije Sommerdag.
Men [illegible] di Sinna Creature
skal Ud ikke giöre. da kan
ikke kan giöres forinden un-
lad man saa saa i Kirkesom
Det ikke bliver giort paa den
saa maa det giöres morgene

Protection for your cows this year against wolves and bears

"I take my cows today to the green pasture, before the Virgin Mary's dearest knee, the victor's stall door. Rise up, conqueror. Take the key in hand. Protect against wolf's teeth, bear claws, and the witch's hand, and for anything that can hurt my cows ...Jerulla, in the name of the Trinity: God the Father, the Son, and the Holy Spirit." Then read the Lord's Prayer. This should be read over salt and given to the cows before they have been fed on New Summer's Day.* But do not give salt to one of the small cows, so it may be sacrificed. He must have one offering. If it is not done on the New Summer's Day, then it must be done the morning after....

---

*April 14, New Summer's Day, marks the transition to the Gregorian calendar that changed the year by eleven days (introduced to Norway in 1700).

Denn skulle Læsis af ehn som
haver Creaturene and fund:
Probatum af: Morten
Fuglesanden forsen
sam alt erar —

...This incantation must be read by the person that takes care of the animals.

Probatum.

By Morten Fuglesande,* for those who believe in it.

---

*Morten Fuglesande is unknown.

at en Drancker skal
aflegge Brendeviinet

---

tag [illegible] tag
[illegible] i [illegible] Brendeviin
i [illegible] lad saa [illegible]
[illegible]

---

at fordrive Vægge Lius

---

tag en Flis af et [illegible]
og [illegible] i Væggene
[illegible] Vægge [illegible]
[illegible]
for [illegible]

---

at Liuis aldrig [illegible]
[illegible]
tag [illegible]
[illegible] gaanden [illegible]

For an alcoholic, to put aside his alcoholic ways

Take three baby mice. Lay them in ½ quart of alcohol for fourteen days. Then let the patient drink the alcohol.

To drive away bedbugs

Take a sliver from a wheel* and set it in the wall or a wall crack where the varmints are. Then they will disappear.

So lice will never thrive on you

Take a human bone from a churchyard and sew...

---

*Wheel *(steile):* a torture instrument used in medieval times. It was designed to mutilate a victim by stretching or disjointing.

At i ölüur Stadens Sinne
tag ikke brent staa-
Ristike Brækedage

---

at Bijeden og Vorstur staa
folk Brijder ud Siuudfast
Bestrÿg den med Bÿgvie
Ols Olie

---

at for Driven Kosterne staa
nu Stigen
tag Tovenbom og ehn
Kriyt og giv samme at
Drik fastende. Probat

...it in your clothes, but do not take a bone on Tycho Brahe days.*

So that boils and growths on people rapidly come to a head

Coat them with vitriol** oil.

To expel a foster from a girl

Take juniper berries.† Cook them. Let her smell and drink of it after she has been fasting.
Probatum.

---

*See footnote on page 49.
** Vitriol: iron sulfate.
†Juniper berries were a well known drug used in the Middle Ages to cause abortions. They are very poisonous.

for en Qvinde, der ligger i
Barns nød, at det skal Komme
4 fraaft.
Tag 40 Stener af feidlille
vand
giv Qvinden det at dri-
kke, saa Komer Fosteret tillige
med Efter bijrden. Qvinden
under staad. —
eller. —
Eller tag too Eg lad den begyn
som Almindelig saadan Kogte
og lad Qvinden sagen
Han gode Stærblade tastende
af dette Vand som Egnen
er Kogt i, saa Efterbarn
skaft skove gaa. dette
skal være nogenskabt
og skiøt ikke skade Qvinden

For a woman who is having a difficult labor, so that the baby will be born quickly

Take two pieces of a white lily root. Give it to the woman to eat. Soon the baby will come and then the afterbirth. The woman will be unharmed.

or:

Take two eggs, let them cook to the consistency of hard-boiled eggs. Have the woman, on a empty stomach, take a couple of good sized spoonfuls of the water that the eggs were cooked in. The birth will then rapidly start. This has been used with very good results and is harmless to the woman.

END OF BOOK TWO

A Witch Trial in 1625

The following is an account of a woman who was burned at the stake in 1625. Ingeborg Økset, interestingly enough, is an ancestor to the Rustad family. She lived on a neighboring farm on the other side of the Gloma River. Ingeborg just happened to be one of the many women from her time who were unjustly sentenced to death based only on the grounds of ridiculous hearsay.

A lengthy court document from the year 1625 describes a case against Ingeborg Økset, who was sentenced to burn at the stake for sorcery and witchcraft. We also learn that her son had suffered that very same dreadful fate just a few months before her.

During the Middle Ages and just before 1700, witches were burned at the stake over the whole of Europe. The worst period for Denmark-Norway was the 1600s. This may have been because of a monarchy that was especially interested in exterminating so-called witches and people who practiced magic. The monarch at that time was Kristian IV, who is otherwise seen by history as being a good king for Norway.

Why was it so easy to get a person convicted on such grounds? First of all, everything points to the fact that the general public was deeply convinced that some individuals knew about sorcery and that it was possible to sell your soul to the devil in return for the ability to perform magic. The common people held fast to these primitive beliefs. This is not so strange when we consider that the thinking of the enlightened few at that time—the clergy serving as royal officials, bailiffs, and sheriffs—did not differ from that of the general public. Incredible as it might seem, all witches were judged according to the old Norwegian laws, royal decrees, and often by "God's own law," the law of Moses.

The maximum punishment under the official law was given to individuals who had magic skills. Bishops, ministers, bailiffs and others had a special responsibility to perform these duties. This law came into effect only eight years before the case against Ingeborg Økset. In order to get some insight into her case, we will take a look at the most important "evidence" that was submitted against her.

In the first place, it has been documented that Ingeborg was turned in by her own sister, Gulluf Krogsti of Løten. Gulluf was executed some time before Ingeborg was accused and pronounced guilty of practicing witchcraft. It was assumed that witches were in league with one another. In such cases, the accused had to inform on others whom they knew to be witches. We must remember here that the accused were tortured in the most beastly ways. This was all legalized by statute in 1617.

Something that proved to be much more serious for Ingeborg was being "exposed" by her oldest son, Peder Lassesen. He was condemned to burn at the stake on January 12, 1625. The charges against him must have been especially grave in the eyes of the authorities because it was not very usual to condemn a man in this way. A man's life was viewed as being worth more than a woman's. And should a man be punished in such a manner, he was often handled in a more "humane" way. He would often be beheaded before being burned at the stake, just like Peder Lassesen. The thought behind burning at the stake was that the

På Kolsås by Theodor Kittelsen

flames had a cleansing effect. The soul would then be saved for the heavenly kingdom.

Part of what Peder had been tried for was repeated in his mother's trial. He was apparently tortured several times. Peder stated that he had come across his mother on Christmas Eve churning butter. He commented that his mother had always been cruel to him. Another time they had ridden together to Givtola the night before Easter, Ingeborg riding a goat and Peder riding a pig. The animals had first been rubbed down with a magic ointment that Ingeborg had in her possession. It was believed that, especially on Christmas Eve and the night before Christmas, witches were out and about practicing their skills.

Givtola was the local version of Brocken, the highest peak of the Harz Mountains in Germany, where it was said that witches would meet with the devil and hold their revels.

Furthermore, Peder stated that he had used witchcraft at the Bånerud farm, after taking advice from his mother on how to destroy Peder Bånerud's beer in the process of brewing.

Ingeborg had supposedly once interfered in what seems to have been a small disagreement between her two daughters-in-law. Gunnor Ingulsdatter (Peder's wife) came to her mother-in-law concerning a half pound of goat cheese that was owed her by Sigrid Rolfsdatter. Ingeborg was so offended that she threatened that it would be lean in the future with goat cheese. That very same year Gunnor had lost all of her goats, an accident that was supposedly due to Ingeborg's witchcraft.

Another charge that was disclosed against Ingeborg involved a previous minister, Lawrits Kristensen. The clergyman had accused her of having bewitched his son, Morten. The minister died around 1610. The rumors surrounding Ingeborg must have circulated some time before a public case was put into motion against her. The minister's son had probably suffered from one or another physical ailment—or more likely from some mental defect. It was believed that such problems were due to witchcraft being used on the afflicted individual.

It appears that Ingeborg's husband, Lasse Gudmundsen, tried to free his wife from these false charges of witchcraft when the rumors began circulating. He had sent the Swedish-born Oluf Vål from Åmot to Sweden to get truthful evidence from a wise woman. She was supposed to clarify Ingeborg's innocence. But Oluf came back with the message that Ingeborg not only knew about the Black Arts but was in fact the shrewdest of them all. Lasse Øxset was so furious that he took back a brass kettle with copper handles that he had given Oluf for taking the trip to Sweden. This point was mentioned several times during the trial and was clearly emphasized as being of great importance. How Lasse behaved during the trial itself is not known. Otherwise, we know that it was extremely difficult for the accused to receive help. In everyone's eyes the accused was already judged to be guilty. Helping an accused person who had sold their soul to the devil could be perceived as being a case of one witch helping another.

It also appears that the prosecutor, in this case Sheriff Nils Eriksen, had a certain trick with his interrogation. He asked if it had been a very long time since she had had dealings with the devil. Ingeborg answered that it had been a long time ago. This was as good as saying that she was guilty of a relationship with the devil. And when she later denied this, she was labeled a two-faced liar.

The trial took place at the court on farm #10 in March 1625. On the jury sat Halvor Grøtting, Laurits Hovin, Tord Hovin, Peder Møystad, Repper Haugen, Jedvard Bjøset, Arne Berger, Anders Løken, Nils Reten, Gudmund Berger, Morten Berger, and Knut Hvarstad. In addition to these "honourable and wellbred" men, those present included Jedvard Sætern, then sheriff of Elverum; Torben Skaktavl, juryman for Opplandede; and his Royal Majesty's sheriff for Hedmark and Østerdalen, Nils Eriksen. Obviously, none of these well respected men had any doubt about Ingeborg's guilt.

A transcript from the last part of the court document in the case against Ingeborg Knutsdatter Økset reads:

> We hereby sentence Ingeborg Knutsdatter for her grave and unchristianlike deeds. Because she has been found to be a two-faced liar, she shall be punished by paying with her life by burning at the stake, and her property, belongings, and real estate shall be forfeited to the king.

En Rådslagning i Kvinne-Foreningen by Theodor Kittelsen

Her last chance for being acquitted was for twelve appointed "honest, respectable, well-bred" women to take an oath together with Ingeborg stating that she was innocent. This was to have taken place ten weeks later, when the case was scheduled to come before the court.

The court assembled again on May 19, 1625. None of the named women (Marit Strand, Sigurd Strand, Gjertrud Strand, Anne Grundset, Åse Gårder, Anne Skulstad, Anne Hovin, Gro Opsal, Gro Lillehov, Oulo Løken, Tora Østerhaug, and Bodil Skjefstad) were willing to take the oath with Ingeborg. On the contrary, they emphasized that they had always heard that Ingeborg was known for her witchcraft, and this was also well known in Elverum's congregation.

Even though Ingeborg denied all guilt, the judge did not hesitate in passing sentence. The accused would be burned at the stake.

How was it possible to conduct such a case against a member of one of the most powerful families in the district? Ingeborg's husband Lasse was the rightful heir and owner of the big farm, Økset. The family's influence is demonstrated by the fact that his father had been the sheriff for many years. The Økset family managed to retain its prominence during the 1600s in spite of the trial. Lasse's brother, Bjorn Grundset, was the sheriff after Jedvard Sætern. Could this whole ordeal have its roots in the disputes within a large family? Concerning this case against Ingeborg, we can see that several family members were involved. First and foremost was her son, the rightful heir; then Ingeborg's two daughters-in-law; and finally Peder Bånered, if his sister was Lasse's sister-in-law. (She was married to Bjørn Grundset.) When we know that sheriff Jedvard Sætern, who was also a jury member in the trial, had a son who was married to the daughter of Bjørn, we can for all practical purposes come to an obvious conclusion. It is also interesting to note that Jedvard Sætern was the son-in-law to the parish Reverend Laurits Kristensen. He introduced the most serious charges against Ingeborg.

On the other hand, it was very usual for the sheriffs and bailiffs to manage such cases with great eagerness when they could seize the opportunity to strike a bargain concerning a farm's real estate—in the king's name. These properties would be forfeited to the king as a fine.

The driving force behind the trials and sentencing of Ingeborg Økset and her son Peder is impossible to determine today. But in any case, this whole account is a dismal revelation of the spiritual darkness in which our forefathers found themselves 370 years ago.

—MAGNE STENER

List of Incantations

Index of Spells

To order copies of this book,
please send full amount plus $5.00 for
postage and handling for the first book and
$1.00 for each additional book.

Send orders to:

Galde Press, Inc.
PO Box 460
Lakeville, Minnesota 55044-0460

Credit card orders call 1-800-777-3454
Phone (952) 891-5991 • Fax (952) 891-6091
Visit our website at www.galdepress.com

Write for our free catalog.

Made in the USA
Monee, IL
15 November 2021

82186997R00102